PRAISE FOR
THE MERCENARY'S DAUGHTER

"A hugely entertaining novel. It pulls you in and doesn't let you go."
—**TOM O'CONNOR**, SCREENWRITER *of THE HITMAN'S BODYGUARD and IRONBARK*

"Big action. Tons of heart. I was hooked from page one."
—**MATT LIEBERMAN**, SCREENWRITER *of THE CHRISTMAS CHRONICLES, THE ADDAMS FAMILY, and FREE GUY*

"One of the coolest and downright fun books I've read in a while."
—**TOMMY WIRKOLA**, WRITER/DIRECTOR *of HANSEL & GRETEL: WITCH HUNTERS and DEAD SNOW*

"Completely compelling. The pages might rip from turning them so fast."
—**NEIL TOLKIN**, SCREENWRITER *of* LICENSE TO DRIVE *and* THE EMPEROR'S CLUB

"Fast-paced and page-turning. I read the entire thing in two days and was sad to see it end."
—**HOLLY KAMMIER**, BEST-SELLING AUTHOR *of KINGSTON COURT, LOST GIRL, & CHOOSING HOPE*

"A dash of Bond, a heaping teaspoon of Lara Croft, and two pinches of sibling rivalry...Crank the heat up in Cuba's criminal underbelly and you have the perfect recipe for an un-put-downable thriller."
—**KAT ROSS**, BEST-SELLING AUTHOR *of THE FOURTH ELEMENT SERIES & THE DOMINION MYSTERIES*

JOE GAZZAM
JESSICA THERRIEN

THE MERCENARY'S DAUGHTER

FROM THE TINY ACORN...
GROWS THE MIGHTY OAK

This is a work of fiction. References to real people, events, establishments, organizations, or locales are intended only to provide a sense of authenticity and are used fictitiously. All other characters, and all incidents and dialogue are drawn from the authors' imaginations and are not to be construed as real.

Printed in the United States of America. For information, address Acorn Publishing, LLC, 3943 Irvine Blvd. Ste. 218, Irvine, CA 92602

www.acornpublishingllc.com

Interior design by Acorn Publishing
Cover design by Damonza

ISBN-13: 978-1-947392-75-5 (hardcover)

ISBN-13: 978-1-947392-74-8 (paperback)

Joe's Dedication:

To Laurie and Rex

Jessica's Dedication:

To Little Tiny Lacey
You will rule the world one day...
And I'll tell people "I told you so."

CHAPTER ONE

SOMETHING BROKE IN ME the day my mother left, and maybe that's why I hardened on the outside, trapping all my hurt behind an iron curtain of indifference.

It wasn't something I could take back. She was the one who'd walked out.

As I sat in the car in front of a stream of cool air, I tried not to think of her. She didn't deserve my thoughts, but it was hard not to wonder where she was. And why? Always why?

What kind of a woman leaves her twelve-year-old daughter without a word? It had been ten years, and I still couldn't come up with an answer.

As I killed the engine to my Jeep, I smothered all thoughts of her and stole a glance in the rearview. Thankfully, I had Dad's full lips and olive skin-tone, but Mom's soft brown eyes still stared back at me through every mirror. I raked my wavy locks of dark brown hair off my forehead.

I was a feminine-looking girl, and as a Marine that always proved to be a mind grenade to the random stranger. Being a soldier wasn't what I would have chosen to do with my life, but I ended up good at it, anyway. Maybe because it was the perfect way to release my rage.

After being let out of juvie for the third time, it seemed like my only option. Well, my only legal option. I'd barely finished my GED so there weren't exactly a slew of Ivy League colleges beating down my door. And frankly, jumping out of planes seemed a lot more fun than the prom I'd missed a few months earlier.

But the real reason I enlisted was Dad. More specifically, it was the look on his face as we left the detention center. He tried his best to hide it, but it was clear he didn't know what else to do. There was a hopelessness in him. The look affected me so much that on the drive home, I'd literally blurted out my plan to join the military like it was a well-thought-out decision. After seeing the life rush back into his eyes, I knew I had to follow through.

Which was one of the reasons I was still in my car while he waited in the bar to see me for the first time in nearly four years. I wasn't looking forward to facing him. Not after what happened.

After three years in the Marines, I'd been one of the first women to make it into Special Ops. I'd almost completed the training. It was a big deal, but just like everything else, I'd found a way to screw it up. At twenty-two I was bounced out on a dishonorable discharge. Great job, Tara.

I blew out a deep breath and grabbed my purse from the passenger seat. It was now or never.

The Miami heat was oppressive, but nothing compared to the desert. Triple-digit temps in full military gear was an entirely different kind of torture. This seemed almost pleasant in comparison. Stepping off the curb, I tugged at my white T-shirt, using it to wipe my forehead, and tucked my cell phone into the back pocket of my ripped jeans as I crossed the cracked, worn parking lot. Combat boots were probably a little much in this weather, but I liked the familiar way they hugged my feet.

As I passed a set of tinted car windows, I caught a glimpse of the tattoo on my upper arm: a picture of an eagle landing on a globe, with the words *Semper Fi* in a banner below. I pulled my sleeve down to cover it up. I'd gotten it with a few other recruits right after getting through boot camp. It seemed like a good idea at the time, but now it only reminded me that most of my closest friends had been lost along the way. I told myself it was a tribute, but the truth was, it made me sick to look at it.

Sidestepping a constellation of crushed glass, I headed to a bar called the Ugly Tarpon Saloon. The door handle stuck to my palm as I gave it a yank, and I wiped the residue on my jeans, opening the door with my foot.

Inside it was pretty much like every other bar in Florida. Sure, there were pockets of culture to be had, but most of the state was painfully nondescript and littered with dumps like this, all fashioned with the same décor: bits of random crap on the walls, maybe a couple pool tables and, of course, the ever-present line of booths packed with overly tan drunks slurping half-empty beers.

The place smelled of dribbled bourbon and tangy old popcorn, but they must have been known for their food, otherwise Dad wouldn't have picked such a scummy place to meet for lunch. Thankfully, I didn't see him at any of the tables, which meant I hadn't kept him waiting.

A woman with tire-streak eyeliner passed me as I plopped down into a vinyl-clad booth, where a light poof of cigarette-stink burped from the cushions. To my right, a group of college boys sat along tipsy-legged tables and gave her their best "How you doin'" chin pump. I ignored them and threw my feet onto the torn cushions as the bartender across the room gave me a hard squint. Only a year over the legal drinking age, I still encountered my fair share of skeptics.

I turned and stared him down, and after a moment, he looked away. Years ago I learned that most people preferred to avoid conflict. I'd been using that to my advantage ever since.

"Hey, Terror," a voice came from the entrance of the bar.

A half smile bent my lips. There was only one person

who called me that.

"Hey, *Harry*," I said, instead of *Dad*, volleying his verbal jab.

Dad was a tall, attractive man with short, graying hair. A salt-of-the-earth sort. The kind of guy who didn't smile much, but when he did, it meant something. And gosh, I missed that smile. I scooted out of the booth as he approached, and just the feel of his strong hug and the smell of Old Spice made me regret staying away for so long.

"Good to see you, *Tara*," Dad finally relented. He had a firm, solid voice, like a heavy door with a good swing, and my smile widened at the sound of it.

"You, too...*Dad*. I've missed your face."

As we sat down, he held up two fingers, signaling the bartender, who gave him an understanding nod. Then came the concerned look I was expecting. I'd seen it a hundred times, but it still made my heart skip with guilt. He rested his elbows on the table, hands cradling his chin, and I braced myself for the oncoming dissection of my life.

"So, how's my little girl?" he asked.

I stiffened. He wanted details about the dishonorable, of course, and I should have thought of something to tell him, but I wasn't ready. No matter whose fault it was, shame still colored my cheeks. Instead, I opted to skirt the issue with a brush off.

"Fine. I guess," I answered.

Thankfully, he didn't push.

"You look good," he said, giving me the full once-over. "Except for the wardrobe."

His words were a hint. No uniform. I pretended not to notice.

"This? It's combat chic."

He let out a deep breath. "Everything's a joke—"

"Dad, really?" I leaned back in the booth. "Do we have to just start right in?"

"I'm your father. Someone's got to do it."

"Really?" I asked, eyeing the bar. "Because I'm twenty-two now, which kinda makes me an adult."

"An adult who's apparently still pushing boundaries."

I sat up straighter, picking up on the disappointment in his voice, but he had no idea what I'd been through. I knew what he was thinking, that I'd gone wild, broken rules. Typical loose-cannon Tara. But it wasn't like that. "The dishonorable discharge...it wasn't..." I couldn't bring myself to tell him. Silence hung in absence of my confession.

"What matters is you're back home." Dad nodded. "Safe. That's all I care about."

I hesitated, feeling the need to explain, but the words died in my throat as I remembered the unwelcome hands on me, the force of strong arms holding me down. The details of my discharge went deeper than I'd let on over the phone. I hadn't even told the whole truth to my superiors. I couldn't prove it, so what was the point? The shame of admitting what actually happened kept me quiet.

Dad shook his head, clearly still dwelling on the topic. "It's a bummer, you know? You could have had a great career. Now what?"

"I'll figure it out," I said, my voice spiking with conviction. "You grew up in the '70s. Wasn't everyone wandering around, trying to find themselves?"

"*I* wasn't."

"'Course not."

Dad frowned, the lines on his whiskered face deepening. "I'm serious, you're just gonna wing it from here? No grand plan?"

"Nope," I flashed him a cheesy fake smile. "The whole world's my oyster."

But I wasn't kidding about the first part. There was no grand plan; there wasn't even a short-term plan. I had no idea what was next. Despite the sardonic front, having no set direction did bother me. I'd banked everything on a career in the Marines and now that was over. I dug my thumbnail into the wooden table avoiding Dad's eyes.

I'd always envied people who knew exactly what they wanted to do with their lives. It was only by chance I'd found the military, but it worked for me. Ironically, the skills I'd acquired on the streets, what had gotten me arrested in the first place, was what made me so good at being a soldier. Funny how when you're one of the "good guys," pointing a gun at someone suddenly makes you the hero. Dad was right to be worried. I didn't know what to do with myself.

"Tara?" he said loudly as the bartender set down two steak sandwiches and a basket of fries.

I looked up and snapped back into focus. "Yeah?"

"I asked if you knew where you're staying?"

"I...thought I might stay at the house," I said, grabbing a fry.

Dad paused, finishing his bite. "Maybe you should stay with a friend."

A friend? The suggestion felt like a betrayal. He was the only one in the world who cared about me and suddenly I wasn't welcome home?

"Why?" I asked in shock, my eyebrows raised in genuine misunderstanding.

"It's been four years. You've barely spoken to Mitch. Never wrote," Dad rubbed the back of his neck. "He's a little...*angsty* about it."

I pressed my lips together and nodded. "No sweat. I should have my pick of homeless shelters, maybe find an unlocked car to crawl into..."

Dad's eyebrows sank into a deep furrow.

"I'm kidding. I've got places I can crash," I said, hiding my hurt feelings with an eye roll. "But come on, does he have to turn into a whiny little girl about everything?" I blew away my wood shavings and looked up. My brother and I had our own issues, but I did miss him. "How's he doing, anyway?"

"Good," Dad answered. "He's enjoying his senior

year, already got accepted to a few colleges. Looks like it'll be MIT, though."

"MIT?"

"I know. There's an admissions counselor who calls every couple of months. They're pretty much courting him at this point."

"Wow," I said, savoring the flavor of real food. "That's great."

"Didn't get those brains from me. Makes me wanna go get a paternity test." We both smiled, and Dad leaned back into the vinyl booth seat. "He's been helping me finish an office I'm putting up in the backyard."

"Really? Kid barely knows how to hold a hammer."

"It's not much, some finish work, light electrical. But you'd be surprised. He's grown up a lot in four years." Dad smirked. "The little brother you left is taller than you now."

"Jeesh, that's hard to swallow."

Dad nodded. "So, listen...I've gotta run, but you're coming to dinner tonight, right? We'll talk more then."

"Oh, so I can come to dinner but can't sleep in my room?"

"I just don't want you guys to fight," he said, throwing some cash on the table and making another gesture to the bartender.

"Us? Fight?"

"Never," he teased. "We'll see how it goes." Dad smiled and pulled keys out of his pocket. "I'm heading back to the office. You need a ride somewhere?"

I laughed. "I have a car, Dad." But the fact that he didn't know made me realize how much distance had grown between us. "I'm gonna see about a job."

"Job? With who?"

"Vince."

Dad's eyes went wide. "Jesus, Tara—"

"It's not like that, Dad," I cut him off. Although I couldn't deny, deep down I was looking forward to seeing my old fling. "Really. Vince is totally legit. He's running his dad's business now. Tropical fish."

He seemed to use every muscle in his body to nod. "I see. Well...if he's turned his life around, then...maybe."

"Yeah, maybe. I think this could be good for me."

As we got up from our booth I felt bad for making him worry. I shouldn't have mentioned Vince.

"Six o'clock, sharp. Pot roast," he said, gripping his keys.

I threw my napkin onto my empty plate. "Yummy. I do love me some pot roast."

"And hey...go easy on your brother," he added. "He has a point. You could have written."

"Don't worry, I'll cut Nancy some slack."

He gave me a warning look. "He hates it when you call him that."

"Uhh, yeah. Why else would I do it?"

Dad reached out for a hug, and I wrapped my arms around him, releasing the burden of all those months overseas and the years away. No matter what issues we had to work out, I was finally home. He kissed the top of my head like he always did, and although I didn't mention how comforting it felt to be near him, how scared and alone I'd been in a world of sand and heat, how hard I'd fought, how much I'd missed him, I didn't pull away.

"Missed you, Kiddo," he said for me. "Glad you're home."

Maybe being discharged was a good thing, I thought as I watched him exit the bar. It was a second chance. A chance to not make my mother's mistakes. I could be a better daughter. A better sister, even. This could be a fresh start.

CHAPTER TWO

I DROVE MY JEEP through the gritty Bird Road Warehouse District, just off the Palmetto expressway, a few miles west of Coral Gables. Among the hulking, concrete buildings, I spotted the place I was looking for, a tin-sided storeroom with two garage doors side by side and the words *Tropical Fish Depot* across the top.

As I parked, I started to second-guess myself. There was a reason I'd left Vince, and let's just say looks weren't the problem. If I chose to go in, chances were I'd be stepping back into a part of my life better left in the past. But...I didn't really have any other leads in terms of jobs, and I *was* really hoping he'd turned his life around.

I ducked under a cracked rolled-up steel door and into a large open space. Inside, enormous tanks full of tropical fish were stacked floor to ceiling. So far so good. The business looked real.

The squeak of my boots against concrete caught the attention of a Cuban man with a snowman's build and a shaved head.

"Can I help you?" he asked.

I gave him a half nod. "I'm looking for Vince. Is he around?"

"Who are you?" The Cuban took a giant sniff and hocked up some phlegm.

"Tell him it's Tara." I watched the man's Adam's apple bob as he downed his own mucus, but I was used to men being gross. "Really? Just gonna swallow it like that?"

The Cuban shrugged, motioned for me to stay put and sauntered off. I knocked on the side of a tank and examined the giant filters. It'd been over a year since I last saw Vince. Back then, he was a low-level contraband specialist. Cars mostly. Steal them here, send them somewhere else. Sometimes vice versa. I'd been boosting cars for Vince since before I had my license. They weren't my best years, but they did teach me how to drive like The Stig.

Back then we were both young and stupid, looking for a way to stick it to the world. It didn't take long for me to get addicted to the rush. And also to Vince. And to the rush of Vince. He was three years older, the good-looking bad boy, and I was the girl who didn't try to fix him. It was all so cliché.

But deep down, he was the real reason I was here. Some fluttery-butterfly part of me hoped we could be together. If he'd sincerely turned his life around, I could help him with his new business. It would give my life focus, purpose. We'd loved each other once. Maybe something was still there.

I turned at the sound of footsteps and saw Vince emerge from the shadows. He had long blond hair and dark brown eyes, a strutting, tan hunk who looked like he'd leapt off the cover of a romance novel. I used to tell him he was prettier than I was. As he approached, I realized I was biting my lower lip and stopped.

"Well, well, well. Look who it is. Back from the dead," Vince said as he pulled me into a hug. He leaned in for a kiss, but I turned my cheek, not wanting to rush into things.

"How you doing, Vinnie?" I asked.

"Can't complain," he said, shaking his head. "You look good. Real good."

My face flushed as old feelings came rushing back. "Thanks."

"What brings you 'round?"

I tucked my hands in my back pockets. "Heard you were doing well. Guess I was hoping for a job."

"A job?" His voice rumbled, low and sexy, like the engine of one of his stolen cars. I tried not to let it shake me.

"Yeah, you know, work in exchange for pay."

Vince paused, his eyes lingering on my lips, and then finally responded. "Sure. Come on."

We walked past more tanks and headed to the back of

the warehouse. Several barking pit bulls were tied to thick chains. The nearest, a white sack of muscle with a missing eye, lunged for me, and I braced for it, but the chain snapped him back.

"Nice pets," I said, taking a reflexive step sideways.

"Most of these fish are rare." He trailed his hand along one of the tanks. "Worth a lotta cash. Can't be too careful."

I looked around, surprised at how big the place was. "Your dad lets you run this whole operation?"

"Please, my dad hasn't stepped foot inside this place in over a year. Been in Europe. Besides, this business is a tax write-off for him. I could run it into the ground, wouldn't make a difference."

"Must be nice."

"Can't pick your parents, but it sure is dope when they turn out to be rich."

"Yeah..."

So maybe he hadn't changed. At least he was cute. I snuck another peek at him. His tight black T-shirt clung to his broad shoulders and chest. Even his jeans seemed to hug his body in all the right places.

"Come on, start talking," Vince said. "Haven't seen you in forever, catch me up. I heard you got busted and then...nothing. You don't call, write. So what's up?"

I crossed my arms and shrugged, choosing to omit the details of my military time. "You know, same old, same old."

"That's it? You vanish like smoke, then show up at my front door with no explanation?"

"I'm just not in the mood for a big reunion," I said, partly lying. "But look...if this is too weird, I can go. I just need a job, a real job, that's all." My stomach tensed as I waited for his answer.

Vince squinted, then motioned to a door. "Naw, it's not weird, come on. I'm always down to help an old friend. Lemme show you my office. I'll get you a W-2."

I nodded, relieved, and followed him inside, holding back the urge to smile. It wasn't until I made it through the door that I felt hands on me. A lot of hands. Several of Vince's men closed in and shoved me back against the wall with a hard thud.

Instantly my head started swimming with memories of my last attack, and my fear built into a wild frenzy. I wouldn't let it happen again.

"Vince!" I screamed, ripping one of my arms free.

But he squeezed between his men and jammed a handgun to my forehead. With a sharp intake of breath, I went still. Terror always gripped my beating heart in those first few seconds of threat assessment, but after years of front-line combat, I'd learned to think and push past it.

"You wearing a wire?" Vince screamed as his men gripped me by the arms.

I didn't answer. Instead, I ran through the motions, calculating how many guys there were, who had guns, their positions and body language. Two big guys holding my arms, handgun in pants. Skinny guy in the corner, unarmed, arms crossed...

"I said—you wired?!" Vince shouted.

"Are you mental?" I seethed through gritted teeth.

Vince reached for my shirt, trying to pull it up, and I saw my chance. I ducked my head away from the aim of his gun and kneed him in the crotch. He instantly heaved and doubled over in pain. Using his men as leverage, I swung my legs up, kicking Vince in the chest with both feet. He crashed into a bookshelf, his handgun skittering across the floor and into the corner. I instinctively lunged for it, but his men yanked me back and slammed me even harder against the wall, knocking the wind out of me.

I went with it, pretending to pass out, and letting my body go slack. Situations like these weren't always about overpowering an opponent. Outsmarting them worked, too. As I sunk to the floor, the big guy on my right loosened his grip on my arm. I ripped it free and snatched the handgun from his pants, twisting away and pointing it at the others.

They pushed forward, and I shot two bullets into the wall next to one of their heads. "Don't test me."

I stared at Vince as he staggered to his feet, more crushed and betrayed than scared of him and his men now that I was free. Whatever residual feelings I'd had for him evaporated instantly. I was an idiot to think he'd changed. Screw him. Once I was out of here, I'd never look back.

"I knew you were a cop," Vince hissed, his eyes ablaze.

"Oh my God." I rolled my eyes and lowered the gun. "Fine. You know what? Here." I charged at Vince and pulled my shirt up from the bottom, keeping my bra covered, but showing enough skin to prove my point. I wasn't wearing a wire. "Happy?" I asked, jaw clenched.

Vince stood back, waving his guys off. "I'm sorry," he said, offering an open-handed shrug. "I've had a couple close calls recently, you know?"

"Okay, and what does that have to do with me?" I glared at him as I fixed my shirt and tucked my hair behind my ears.

Vince threw his hands up. "You show up out of nowhere and don't tell me where you've been when I ask what you've been up to. What was I supposed to think?"

I shook my head, regretting the decision to come here. "Look, I told you, all I wanted was a job."

Vince looked away embarrassed. "Sorry, all right?"

"I guess news of *your* reform's been greatly exaggerated," I said, the disappointment a heavy weight in my chest. "So what's the deal here? Fish are cover. What's the real cargo?"

Vince hesitated, still clearly suspicious.

I widened my eyes. "Seriously? I'm not a cop."

"Pharmaceuticals mostly," he said, finally giving in. "Whole car gig had too much downside. This is way easier." He moved to sit on the edge of his desk. "Look, I really can hook you up with a job. My shit's global now."

"You know, I really hoped you'd gotten your act together. We could have..." I pressed my lips together and swallowed down the tightness in my throat. "If you get caught, your dad could go down with you."

I couldn't help but think of the conversation I'd just had with my own father. *He* was the one who'd tried to stay in touch. He was the one who cared about me. I couldn't go down this path with Vince and disappoint him again.

Vince shrugged, not giving it a second thought. "Yeah, whatever. I won't get caught."

"You really don't give a crap about anyone but yourself, do you?"

"Tara," Vince said as I turned away. "Don't be like that. I said I was sorry."

"Sorry?" I stopped, flooded with emotion all over again. "Vince, you held a gun to my head."

"Don't be so sensitive. I wouldn't have done anything."

"Whatever," I said, sliding between two of his men. "Bye, Vince."

As I walked away I realized I was still gripping the gun, my knuckles white, as angry tears threatened to blur my vision. I released the clip and slid it into a random corner before picking up my pace and leaving the warehouse. There was no way Vince was going to see me cry.

CHAPTER THREE

AS I PULLED UP to my childhood home, with its dated brown siding straight out of the 1970s, my stomach twisted with equal parts dread and nostalgia. Mitch was shooting hoops in the driveway and turned as I parked, but he didn't wave or smile. Dad was right, he had gotten taller. My little brother was long and lanky, and just starting to grow out of those awkward teenage years, but the angst was still there, apparently.

"What? Four years and no wave?" I joked as I approached.

He dragged a hand through his untidy blond hair and ignored me, shooting a free-throw. The ball bounced against the garage door and rolled back to him.

Just as I was about to guilt him with another jab, a BMW M3 convertible pulled into the driveway across the street. In the passenger seat sat Nora, the seventeen-year-old blonde Mitch had been in love with since he was five.

"Oooo. There's your girl," I said following his gaze.

"Shut up," Mitch responded.

His eyes seemed to narrow at the barrel-chested muscular guy behind the wheel, who sported a puka shell necklace, bad tribal tattoos, and a backwards baseball cap—the full douche-bag tuxedo.

"Who's the hunk?" I joked.

"Jake," Mitch answered. "Her boyfriend."

Nora got out of the car, her tan legs lifted by strappy wedges and topped by a white miniskirt. She ran around to the other side of the convertible and gave Jake a kiss. He pulled her halfway through the window, smacking her on the butt.

"He seems like a real catch."

"What does she see in that tool?" Mitch asked.

"What does it matter? If it wasn't him it'd be somebody else. You haven't had the balls to ask her out since you were in first grade. What do you expect?"

Mitch dribbled a few times, but still wouldn't look at me. "Maybe you're right."

"Why don't you just tell her how you feel?"

"Seriously? Are you really giving me the girl talk right now?"

Suddenly, Jake jammed his car into gear, reversed out of the driveway and pulled back into the street. He took one look at Mitch, hocked up a big loogie, and spit it in our direction, then floored the BMW, zooming around the corner out of view.

My upper lip curled in disgust. "Charming."

As Mitch watched Nora enter her house, I took that as my cue to leave. I could feel him stewing over it all, and if I stayed, I knew his irritation would boil over into a fight with me.

"See you inside," I said, heading for the door.

THE HOUSE HADN'T changed much. It still had the same smell. Like warm dusty carpet and clean laundry. I peered around the living room. The old, worn leather couch still sat against the center wall. The floor remained covered by the hideous brown shag I'd begged my dad to rip up for years. But somehow it was all immediately comforting. Between deployment and special ops training, it'd been nearly four years since I'd been back.

As I walked through, I paused at the mantel and let my eyes drift across the line of pictures. I recognized some of them. The one with Mom and Dad on their wedding day. Another of me at ten years old playfully wrestling Mitch to the ground. Mom's head was tossed back in laughter, her blonde hair spilling down her back. It didn't make sense to me that Dad kept pictures of her up in the house. She was gone. She didn't deserve a place on the mantel.

The next was of me, Mitch and Dad. Mom conspicuously absent, as if someone had simply Photoshopped her out. But the last one was recent, Mitch and Dad celebrating a track and field win. Mitch held up a trophy of a tiny golden man jumping midair. This time, I was the one missing. A twinge of guilt knotted in my gut. I couldn't help but compare myself to Mom.

But my absence was different. I didn't abandon my family. I left to join the military and begin my life as an adult.

Despite my excuses, I knew Dad was right. I should have called. I should have come home when I was on leave, but the real world became a foreign place to me when I was overseas. I saw it as a web of temptation enticing me to go AWOL. Best to cut it off cold turkey.

As I headed to my room, I noticed the hallway shelves lined with Mitch's achievements. Track medals and long jump trophies were displayed in tiered levels. I'd missed so much.

At least I was back now. I'd make up for it.

"Hey, you made it," Dad said, coming into the room wearing an apron with the words *Real men wear aprons* across it.

"Do they? Really?" I nodded at the phrase.

He smiled. "Come on, I've got someone I want you to meet."

I hesitated, not expecting to have to share my homecoming with anyone, especially someone new. Without much of a choice, I followed Dad into the kitchen. Behind the center island an attractive, dark-skinned woman in her late forties stood fixing a salad. Her black hair was wrapped in a bun and deep dimples sank into her cheeks as she smiled, her face lighting up at the sight of me.

Dad motioned. "Tara, this is Sasha, my girlfriend."

Sasha wiped her hands on a towel. "Well, hello there," she said, coming around the island for an awkward hug. I pulled away, stiff and uncomfortable. Dad never mentioned a girlfriend. I wasn't sure how I felt about it. "So," I glanced at Dad, "am I meeting my new mom, or is this like a..."

Sasha laughed and waved a hand. "I'm not anyone's mom."

"Sasha works with me at the office," Dad said, picking up a knife to cut tomatoes.

"Cool." I bobbed my head, trying to think of something else to say. "Look at you, Pop. Still got it."

"He's got something, not sure what it is, though," Sasha said, grabbing a bottle of wine from the counter. "Would you like a glass?"

"I'll have one," Mitch said, appearing in the doorway, sweat dripping from his forehead.

Dad laughed. "Not on my watch."

Despite Mitch's earlier irritation with me, I smiled at him. "So, how've you been?"

He avoided eye contact. "Oh, so now that you're home, you suddenly care?"

"Ouch..." An endless stream of snarky comebacks spilled into my head, but I held my tongue. I wasn't here to fight with him. The next couple of seconds passed with embarrassing slowness, until I finally turned to Sasha. "So, can I help you guys with anything?"

She pointed to a cutting board and a giant mound of potatoes. "You can chop these up. We're going to sauté them."

Dad grabbed Mitch. "I gotta throw the steaks on, and you've gotta get in the shower. Let the girls talk."

As they left, I picked up a long knife, absent-mindedly flipping it in the air and catching it by the handle.

Sasha cocked an eyebrow. "Know how to handle a knife. They teach you that in the Marines?"

I laughed. "No. Rotations in the mess hall. It's been a while, but I've sliced more potatoes than I wanna think about."

"I find the military so fascinating. Forgive me if this is rude, but...did you see any, you know, *action*?"

Action. My eyebrows shot up. People always made it sound like I'd been off shooting the next Marvel movie or something.

As the seconds passed, I lost myself to memories of Iraq. The ear-splitting crack and ping of bullets. The vacant stare of my closest friend, Dobbs, as he lay there motionless and bloody in the dirt. Just gone. I could still feel the shaky heartbeats, the panic, the urge to run. Still remember the way my body rebelled against the decision to stay and fight.

"Um." I stared at the counter, miles away. "Yeah. A little."

Sasha threw the salad contents into a bowl. *What a luxury,* I thought, *fresh salad.*

"I'm sorry." She cleared her throat. "Do you mind if I ask what happened? Why you left?"

"You mean, why I was dishonorably discharged?" I turned to look at her, gauging her reaction, and could tell by her sad expression that she already knew. "I'm assuming Dad told you."

She shrugged and nodded, her mouth twisting into a sympathetic smile.

I swallowed, choking back the memory. It seemed to follow me no matter where I went.

"I...shot a guy in the foot," I answered, keeping the whole truth locked up inside me. "A Captain, actually."

Sasha cocked her head. "Right. Now I need the whole story."

Didn't everybody? But what business was it of anyone's what those men did to me? They were so careful not to rip clothes or leave marks. And with two against one there wasn't much I could do. Two ranking officers' word against mine. I was lucky one was stupid enough to leave his gun within reach. He was lucky all I shot was his foot.

"Being an enlisted girl is, like, no problem at all, ninety nine percent of the time. But there's always that one percent, you know? We were on a special forces training patrol and got separated from the rest of our squad. The two guys I was with came onto me, and when I said no, they got...rough. So I got rougher."

I didn't know why I told her. Maybe because she was a stranger who wouldn't be devastated by the truth, but it felt good to say it out loud. The relief of admitting it to another person felt like sharing the burden and proved it wasn't just something I'd imagined. What happened to me was wrong, and it wasn't my fault. But the humiliation of that frightening, fragile moment still ached like a fresh wound.

"Oh my god, that's horrible." Sasha froze with the salad bowl in her hands. "It's not right, you should—"

"It was my word against theirs," I interrupted. I threw the diced potatoes into a large skillet on the stovetop. "And since one was a decorated Captain, and with the military having all their issues with sexual assaults...it was easier for them to kick me out than admit what really happened."

"Does Harry know?"

I winced. "Not exactly." I'd thought about telling him, but it wouldn't change anything. "It's just easier...for both of us this way. I'd rather him think it's 'typical screw-up Tara' than upset him with the images of me being assaulted. Being a screw-up is something I can fix, but the truth will never stop torturing him."

Sasha's shoulders slumped. "I'm so sorry."

"Yeah, kinda ruined my whole career path," I said,

trying not to sink back into the memory. "I guess now I'll have to become an assassin or something. I don't know." I flashed a playful smile at Sasha and lit the burner. "Not sure yet."

WE ATE DINNER QUIETLY, the four of us studying our steaks as silence stifled the room. I glanced at Mitch, who drank from a tall glass with some sort of green gooey shake inside, but his expression remained cold and distant. Even Dad and Sasha wouldn't look up from their plates.

"So, Sasha, you and my dad do the same thing?" I finally asked, deciding enough was enough.

Sasha dabbed at the corners of her mouth with a napkin. "Me? No, I'm just a rep. Harry designs the slides, I run around and get manufacturers to buy them."

"Slides for like, dishwashing machines and stuff, right?"

"Exactly, dishwashers, mostly." Sasha smoothed her napkin back over her lap. "But some industrial items too."

Dad turned to me. "Speaking of work, how'd that job interview with Vince go?"

I scratched my head. "Um...I don't think that's gonna work out. He's actually cutting back, not hiring," I answered, spearing a seasoned potato. "But there's an installation job I heard about. An alarm company."

Mitch laughed a little too loudly. "Hey, do what you

know."

"Mitch—"

I waved Dad off. "It's okay. If he doesn't get it out, we'll never get past it."

"Oh, we've been past it," Mitch muttered. "In fact, we've been past it for four years now."

I bit the inside of my cheek, knowing what he was getting at, and immediately my defenses went up. I wasn't Mom.

"Mitch, I joined the Marines," I snapped, unable to hold back. "I didn't take off."

Mitch dropped his fork on the table, and looked me in the eyes. "Call it whatever you want, but you couldn't stay out of jail, and then when you had no other choice, you bailed." He caught himself and turned to Sasha, then to Harry. "I'm sorry."

"It's okay," Sasha said with an empathetic smile.

"I thought I could deal with this, but..." Mitch grabbed his glass of green goo, headed out the sliding glass doors and disappeared into the backyard.

I leaned back in my dining chair, a little shocked by how deep-set his anger seemed to be. He'd always had a short fuse, but he wasn't a grudge holder. Usually a few jokes would lighten his mood and we'd be over it.

I laughed uncomfortably. "So, that went well."

It didn't take me long to go after him. I stepped into the backyard, past a ring of shrubs, and made my way up to the nearly completed office Dad had mentioned. The only thing left to do was some finish work and a little painting.

Eventually I found Mitch on a plastic lounge chair by our small kidney-shaped pool. I knew he heard me coming, but he didn't turn. Instead, he took another sip of his green drink.

"What do you want?" His deflated tone broke my heart a little. I hadn't realized he'd been so upset about my leaving.

I plopped down on the empty lounge chair beside him and looked up at the night sky. A low-hung sliver of moon sat patiently behind gray clouds, as hazy as the heart of an ice cube.

"So, you get your acceptance letter yet?"

"Spare me. I'm not in the mood for small talk and you're horrible at it anyway."

I exhaled and nodded. After a few moments, I pulled out a thin-pressed silver necklace. There was a medallion at the end, a picture of a matronly woman with a halo, staring down at a child. Saint Anne. The patron saint of families and children. I rubbed my thumb against the smooth back, the way I'd done so many times in Fallujah. No matter how bad things got, it always reminded me that somewhere out there I had my family, and if I ever made it back, they'd be there.

I held it toward Mitch. "Still have yours?"

"No. Why would I? It didn't work."

I stared off across the yard, up over a long row of palm

trees, their tops clumped like a dragon's back. Leaning forward, my boots bruised footprints into the grass, and I slowly slipped the necklace back under my shirt. "Look, I know—"

Mitch shot to his feet. "You don't know anything," he said, flinging the words like claps of thunder.

My head hung in defeat. "Sit down and talk to me, okay?"

Instant anger swept across his face. "No, you don't get to control this situation."

"I'm not trying to."

"You always do. You do whatever you want, whenever you want. You always have. So, don't pretend you give a crap about this family."

"I *do*."

"Bullshit," Mitch yelled.

"Mitch, come on. I did what I had to do." My words felt empty in the silence, like he was beyond my reach. "What did you expect? That we'd be pen pals?"

"I expected you to get your freaking life together and be here. For me. For Dad. You just drove your life into the ground and used the military to get out of it all. And don't act like you joined because you *believe in this country* or whatever. Like you're some sorta hero."

"I'm not saying I—"

"And no, we didn't need to be pen pals, but how about a phone call? *Something*."

I shot up to my feet and stepped toward him. "You

think I didn't try? Every time I sat down to call I felt like I was saying goodbye. I couldn't get that deep. I couldn't do it, okay? Have you even thought, for a second, how *I* felt? I watched friends die. There were times I didn't think I'd make it. Isn't that payment enough for all the dumb shit I did?"

Mitch stared at the dark grass at his feet. "It's always about you. No one else matters because you've got it worse."

I exhaled a sigh. Maybe he was right. In pushing him away to protect myself, I'd made him relive the worst part of our childhood. "Would it help if I said I was sorry?"

He shrugged.

"I'm sorry," I said, really meaning it.

He shook his head, and I could see all the hurt I felt when Mom left in the way he looked at me. "I'll get over it."

As he turned to go back inside, I watched him walk away, wishing I could redo the last four years.

"Thanks for not making this weird," I yelled after him, wincing at the sound of the sliding glass door slamming shut.

CHAPTER FOUR

MITCH, DAD AND I walked Sasha to the door. The drama of the night still permeated as Sasha gave me a hug goodbye. I could feel it in the stiff way she held her shoulders. When we separated, Sasha and Dad's cell phones rang at the exact same time. They gave each other a vague conspiratorial glance, before muting their ringers.

"Must be work. I'll see Sasha out," Dad said, as they both quickly left the house.

I moved to the window, opening the blinds a hair to see them both on their phones. What kind of an appliance design company had emergencies after 8 p.m.? The two of them were engaged in animated conversations, and I squinted, wishing I could hear what they were saying, but eventually gave up and closed the blinds.

I slumped down onto the couch, waiting for Dad to

come back and explain. Mitch flipped on the TV. Details of the Prague embassy attack were all over the news. It had happened days after my discharge.

A new kind of weapon was involved. It wasn't a typical bombing. There was no outward explosion, but rather some kind of *implosion.* The news camera flashed to a helicopter view. Overhead, a scorched patch of earth stretched on for entire city blocks.

This was big. I hadn't heard from Tibbens or BT, two of my Marine buddies, since I'd left. I wondered what repercussions it had on them. They'd finished training. Maybe they were there.

For a good five minutes, Mitch and I watched in silence.

"Can you believe this?" I asked. "The buildings are just...gone. I—"

Mitch switched the channel without answering, finally settling on a show about how the universe was created, and cranked up the volume.

I let out a heavy, frustrated sigh. While some things had changed, one thing hadn't, he still knew how to piss me off. I pressed my lips together, trying to avoid another blow out. Thankfully, Dad came back through the front door.

"So...that was the office," he said, clearing his throat. There was a dark brown envelope under his arm. "There's an emergency at our Beijing plant. They made this drawer slide 1/4 inch, instead of 1/2...Never mind, point is, I've got to visit the plant and get things back on track."

I stood, my mind swimming with suspicion. "Wait. You're leaving?"

"I'm afraid so. Tonight, in fact, just for a few days. I need to put out a few fires and then I can head back."

What he was saying didn't make senses. Nobody flew out in the middle of the night to fix dishwasher slides. Before I could interrogate him further, Mitch looked up from his show.

"Where's *she* staying?" he asked.

Dad hesitated, as if suddenly remembering the conversation we'd had earlier. I waited to see what he'd say.

"Here. If that's okay with you," he answered.

"It's not my house," Mitch said, turning back to the TV.

Dad cocked an eyebrow at me, and I flashed him a cheesy smile in response, hoping I didn't have to go searching for a free couch this late.

"All right then. You two, try not to kill each other."

AS DAD FINISHED packing, I stepped into his room, lingering by the doorway. His bag was meticulously organized, everything rolled and folded and separated into different sections. Much like him, everything was pristine and in perfect order.

"Do you need a lift to the airport?" I asked, hopeful he'd take the bait. The whole Beijing story seemed made up. If I could catch him in his lie, maybe he'd tell me what was really going on. "I could drive your car and drop you off."

"No, I've got a ride. Thanks."

"Okay, come on," I said, unable to hold back. "Tell me the truth. You think I really believe you're flying out in the middle of the night for a dishwasher emergency?"

He zipped up the small suitcase, and stared at it for a moment. "Tara. Do you think I'd really leave if I didn't have to?"

I shook my head. "That doesn't answer my question. Are you trying to track down Mom or something? Why won't you tell me?"

He stopped and stepped closer to me, putting a hand on each of my shoulders. "Honey." He looked into my eyes with a sad downturn of his lips. "I know you've been through a lot, but I promise, this is work. It's 8 a.m. over there. The plant just opened."

I pressed my lips together, feeling guilty for doubting him. Maybe the military had skewed my view of reality, turning me into a one of those paranoid veterans most people thought were crazy.

"I'll be back before you can say Tallahassee." He turned away to grab his bag, letting it go. "Oh, and about your brother. He'll get over it. Just try and take it easy on the kid."

"I will," I said mechanically, still lost in thought.

"I guess what I'm getting at is...he tends to bottle

everything up. Try to let the steam out a little at a time so he doesn't explode. Know what I'm saying?"

I nodded, but as Dad started to head away, I couldn't ignore the nagging shard of guilt in my heart. We hadn't really had the chance to talk. Not one on one. "I know I've made things difficult," I blurted out.

Dad turned. "What?" he asked, thrown off by my words.

"I just don't know...how to fix my mistakes," I admitted. It had been so long since I'd opened up to him, I felt myself freezing up. I made fists of my hands and my nails dug into my palms. "I wish I could—"

"Listen to me." He stepped closer again and lifted my chin with his knuckle, looking me in the eyes. "I'll always love you. And I know Mitch loves you, too."

Something about being home made me feel so lost again. I didn't want him to leave.

"What should I do?" I asked.

"Just be there. That's all."

"Right," I said. Although I wasn't quite sure being here was enough. Mitch wasn't exactly happy I was staying. "Do you have to go? Isn't there someone else who can handle this one?"

"Hey, when I get back, I'll take some time off and we'll log in some major father-daughter time, okay? I'm willing to make an effort if you are."

I nodded. "Yeah, I'd like that."

"Everything's going to be fine. I'll be back in a few

days." He kissed me on the forehead and pulled me in for a one-armed hug.

"Okay," I said, forcing a smile. "Well, have a good flight. And be careful, okay?"

As he disappeared down the hallway, I rubbed my face with both hands. I was looking forward to being the better daughter, to spending time with Dad and proving to him I could manage without the military. Now I was just stuck with Mitch, whose life's mission was to poke me with a stick until I exploded.

Cue the sarcastic eye-roll—this should be fun.

THAT NIGHT MY dreams were warped with details of the Prague attack and the ghosts of friends I'd lost in Fallujah.

As I drifted off to sleep, I found myself watching a short man with dark skin, darker hair and a full beard through a peephole in an adjacent hotel room. He dropped a surprisingly slender missile launcher into a fiberglass carrying tube, then slipped the bungee-cord strap of the tube over his shoulder and headed for the door.

"He's making his move," a deep and distant voice crackled into my earpiece.

I glanced at the Glock in my hand, realizing I was the special agent in charge of neutralizing the threat.

"I'm on it," I answered back.

Emerging on the top floor of a luxury resort, I spotted the man charging to the elevator. Beads of sweat ran down his back as he hazarded a glance over the railing, down into the atrium.

The suites were set in a circle and framed the lobby, which highlighted an enormous aquarium, five stories below, that held a hundred thousand gallons of sea water and two hundred different species of fish. The man jerked back as the elevator announced its arrival with a dainty ding. He lurched inside. The doors slapped shut behind him.

I barreled forward in a dead sprint, racked the chamber of my handgun and leveled it toward the elevator, but I was too late.

My earpiece crackled again. "Tell me you have eyes on the target."

I slid against the railing, catching sight of the dark-haired man riding the glass elevator down to the lobby, and answered into my tiny collar microphone. "Not for long."

The voice in my ear was desperate. "I've got no one else in proximity."

"Understood," I answered. With a quick swing of my leg, I stepped over the railing.

I sized up the aquarium below. This was an atrocious option, but the only one left. I ceased all thought, gritted my teeth and jumped. My stomach left me as I dropped the five stories and struck the serene water, the weight of my body crashing into the floor of the tank with a hard slam.

The impact was the equivalent of being hit by a car, and for a moment I blacked out, but the cold water jerked me back into consciousness. I stirred, looked around. The lip of the aquarium was thirty feet up. I could swim for it, but it would eat more time. Instead, I jammed my gun against the tank and fired. The enormous glass wall transformed into a beautiful spider web, then disintegrated. Glass detonated outward, vomiting thousands of gallons of water into the lobby.

Hotel patrons screamed and scattered as I rolled out onto the floor along with hundreds of squirming fish. As I scrambled to my feet and burst outside, I spotted the dark-haired man heading for the fire escape. Pushing past the searing pain in my leg, I clenched my jaw, and made a final limping sprint toward the target. But as I reached the staircase, the man disappeared onto the roof of the building and out of sight.

Seconds later, the missile launched across the blue plane of sky above, like a distant jet leaving a smoke trail.

My heart seized and I closed my eyes. I'd failed...

Like a ghost, the dream carried me to the scene, where a large crowd of people gathered in front of the U.S. Embassy in Prague. They would be completely vaporized by what happened next. Somehow, I'd seen it before. I knew it was coming. Every cell in their bodies would collapse and disintegrate instantly. And any remaining trace of their existence would be blown away by the ensuing summer wind.

As they milled about, their last moments passed without thought. Not one of them knew it was the end.

White clouds migrated across a wide sky. A young couple leaned against the wrought iron Embassy gate and fell into each other's arms. I recognized the boy. His short sandy curls were grown out and his cherub face had thinned some. I'd met Dobbs a few days after joining the Marines. He'd barely made it, huffing and puffing his way through boot camp, but he was funny and friendly. As outsiders, we stuck together.

In the dream, Dobbs and his girlfriend stopped lip-locking for a moment to take a picture of themselves with the flapping red, white and blue flag behind them. The girl curled a piece of hair behind her ear and offered a well-practiced smile. As Dobbs extended his arm to take the selfie, the shoulder-launched missile struck the side of the building with an eruption that completely astounded the air.

The result was unexpected. The missile didn't explode, but rather imploded, causing the entire embassy to collapse inward. Concrete walls sucked together as the building's metal structure folded like a closing flower bud. Trees were ripped from their roots and parked cars tossed like toys flicked by the finger of an angry child. Everything in a two-hundred-yard radius crumpled like a beer can as it was pulled into the vortex. And at the very moment of critical mass, the implosion instantly rubber-banded back out at equal velocity, screaming in every direction at once. In a millisecond, all that remained was the resulting tidal wave of dust, ash and debris.

And then, nothing but silence.

"Dobbs!"

I woke, screaming, hunched against the side of my bed, the image of Dobbs lying feet from me under a cloud of raining dirt.

"Dobbs!"

We'd lost him in Fallujah, and even in sleep, I couldn't escape the memory of the last time I saw his face.

As the dream faded, and I began to snap out of the trauma of reliving the loss of my friend, I sank against the wall. My shoulders shook as I cried and my chest worked hard to keep up. I knew the moment it happened that his death would haunt me. I just never imagined it would follow me home.

The sound of my bedroom door creaking made me look up. Mitch was there, standing in his plaid pajama pants half illuminated by the moonlight.

"You okay?" he asked, his voice quietly concerned as he watched from a distance.

I didn't know how long he'd been standing there.

"Yeah," I said, my hiccupped breath slowing back to normal.

I expected him to leave, but he came in and sat next to

me on the floor.

"What happened?" he asked, looking over at me. As our eyes connected, a moment of understanding and forgiveness passed silently between us.

"In the dream or in Fallujah?" I returned my focus to the side of my bed, still haunted by the images.

"Both, I think," he answered.

I rested my head against the wall, and let out a deep sigh.

"My best friend in the service was a guy named Jeff Dobbs. He shouldn't have enlisted. He wasn't cut out for it." Somehow, I still carried around the guilt for not convincing him to go home early on, like maybe he would have if it wasn't for me. He knew I'd be alone without him, and deep down I knew it too, which is why I never pushed it. "We were headed out on an easy routine mission to sweep the area for threats in the Humvee. I argued with him about the window seat and made him sit in the middle."

My head sank into the top of Mitch's shoulder. Despite our issues, there was still an underlying closeness between us. He put on a hard front when he was mad, but through all the mistakes I'd made, Mitch had never failed to be there for me when I needed him. I wished I could say the same.

"We hit an IED," I finished. "He didn't make it."

Mitch rested his cheek against my messy mop of hair, his silent comfort a gentle balm to soothe my damaged heart.

CHAPTER FIVE

AFTER DAD LEFT, I spent my time binge-watching TV and not getting dressed. At first, sleeping in until 11 a.m. felt freeing, but eventually it just became severely depressing. As I rolled off my mattress in the same extra-long T-shirt I'd been wearing around the house for the past two days, I decided enough was enough. Time to get it together.

I slid into a fresh pair of cut-off jean shorts and a tight black tank. Maybe I'd see about that Alarm job today. My autopilot routine kicked in, and in less than a minute I made the bed in perfect Marine fashion with ultra-tight corners and razor-sharp folds. As I pinched a stray hair from the pillow, it dawned on me that I didn't have to make my bed like that anymore. Ever again. I was now a civilian.

I considered yanking the sheets back out in protest, but instead, headed down the hall and into the kitchen. Putting my foot on the counter and stretching my hamstring, I noticed my long legs were still cut with sharp lines of muscle from forced twenty-mile hikes sporting fifty-pound gear. Special Forces training had been such a day-in, day-out relentless grind, I almost felt guilty for letting myself get lazy.

I lowered my leg and shook my tank, trying to fan the heat from my body. It had to be in the nineties already, and because Dad refused to use the AC, the air hung thick and humid like the inside of a greenhouse. As I poured cold coffee into a glass of ice, I heard hammering. Outside the kitchen window Mitch was attempting to put trim around the door of the backyard office. I watched, smiling to myself as he tried to hold the wood in place and hammer the nail at the same time. It wasn't going well.

My bare feet brushed the thick, shag carpet as I padded back to my room. I eyed my combat boots. They stared at me from the corner like a pair of old neglected friends. Considering the heat, I stepped into a pair of sneakers instead and headed outside where Mitch was still struggling with the trim. I silently grabbed the other end and secured it.

He paused, but continued to hammer. "Finally decided to get dressed?"

"Shut up. I've earned a day or two of lazy." When he finished, I grabbed another piece. "So, MIT, huh? You must be psyched."

We hadn't worked through our fight, but Mitch seemed to have the worst of it out of his system. At least he was back to acknowledging me.

"Yeah. That's what Dad says too, 'I must be so excited about it.'"

"Thought MIT was every nerd's fantasy."

"Not this nerd." He took a minute to hammer then reached for his water bottle. "I mean, yeah, it's a great school. But twenty-four-seven classes, lab, study hall, and the library. I finally get out of high school and *that's* my next four years?"

I watched him drink as the sun warmed my bare shoulders. "What else would you want to do?"

"I don't know. I thought about joining the Marines for a second, but Dad killed that pretty quick."

I laughed. "You? A Marine?"

"Why not?"

I had a million reasons why not. A million burns, a million put-downs, but I stopped myself. Why not be the cool older sister for once and extend the olive branch? "You know, you're right," I said, handing him another piece of trim. "Why not?"

"You think I could?" he asked, picking through his small pile of nails.

I tried to imagine him infiltrating enemy camps in the desert, sweat dripping into his eyes, shaky fingers on the trigger of an M16 and bullets waiting around every corner.

Not a chance.

"I mean, it's brutal, but yeah...I think so," I lied.

Mitch gave a confident nod as he hammered in the last nail completing the door frame, and I smiled at his back.

THE LATE AFTERNOON sun turned the office into a sweatbox. After finishing the trim, Mitch and I moved inside to paint, working in complete silence.

I glanced at him and refilled my tray of paint with a glistening eggshell white. Just tell him everything, I thought to myself. Tell him that you know you've been a crappy sister and put the family through years of grief. That you want to fix things and want him to be your little brother again. Just stop being so closed off and tell him.

"Long, even strokes," Mitch said, breaking the silence. "I want it perfect for Dad when he gets back."

"Long and even. Got it."

I zoned out to the rhythmic sound of our paint rollers sticking against the drywall.

"You know what today is, right?" Mitch asked.

"Ummm...Thursday?"

Mitch stopped painting.

"Mom's birthday."

I let out a breath, but kept working. "So?"

"I've decided I'm done being mad at her. What's the point?"

"Oh sure, let *her* off the hook," I scoffed, my voice thick with sarcasm. "I join the military and you lose it. But *Mom*, all she did was cut out and abandon her kids. I mean…I guess that's cool."

"Really? Gonna make this about you?"

I sighed, refocusing on my section of the wall. The dim light and paint fumes were giving me a headache.

"She loved us," Mitch continued with his point. "I know she did. I know whatever reason she had for leaving, it had to be a good one."

I redipped my roller. "She had a reason all right. She didn't wanna take care of two little kids anymore."

"I don't believe that."

"Yeah, well, you believed in Santa Claus till you were ten."

Mitch tried not to smile, but did. "That just proves you and Dad were good liars."

"Ten years old! And you're supposed to be the smart one."

"Shut up," Mitch said, holding his roller out like a weapon.

I turned. "I will jam your entire head into that paint can."

Mitch slowly lowered his arm and both of us had a good laugh.

Now's the time, I thought. *Tell him you're sorry. He's in a good mood.* I looked up, ready to spill my guts but froze as Sasha suddenly appeared in the doorway. The woman's face was completely ashen and her expression reeked of devastation. My chest hurt before she even said a word.

"Hey, Sasha," Mitch said, spotting her. He saw the look on her face too and dropped the roller into the tray.

Sasha walked inside, avoiding eye contact with either of us. "I...don't know how to tell you this. I just came from the office."

I could already feel the loss lurking in the still air around me. "Tell us what?"

"Your father..." Sasha said, her voice cracking slightly.

My heart stuttered. I couldn't take it. Not Dad. "What about him?"

"Your father...he's dead."

I stared at her in disbelief, the wind so completely knocked out of me I couldn't respond.

"What?" I finally managed, though I was hardly listening. It felt like someone had grasped the soft lining of my stomach and squeezed it like a washcloth.

"There was a car accident on the way to the plant. It was raining and the roads on the outskirts of Beijing aren't very good. He was going over a bridge and lost control. The car went into a river and..." Sasha got choked up and let her words fade to silence.

My eyes filled and my whole body ached. I couldn't breathe. Beside me, Mitch fell back against the wet, freshly painted wall, marking up its slick surface as he slid to the floor. As he sat there, emotionless, completely devoid of life, I felt the dim spark of rage inside me ignite, building into a wildfire of grief.

THE SUN BURNED a deep red, fighting in vain to stay above the horizon as darkness made its final sweep through the neighborhood. The streetlights had not yet flickered on. Moths lay in wait, ready to rush them as the sky turned gunmetal gray.

Inside the house, I sat at the dining room table. I had cried all I could cry, until I felt like a sponge left out in the sun for days. The whole thing was so strange and sudden, I couldn't completely accept it. Dad's death lingered like an unreachable ache that couldn't be soothed. Tormenting me. Something wasn't right about it. I'd known it in my gut the minute they'd received the simultaneous phone calls.

I stared out the sliding glass doors at Mitch sitting alone in the dark. I could just make out the shape of his body. He was still in the office, sitting on the floor against the wall, in the exact same spot.

Sasha approached the table with two bowls of freshly made spaghetti and set one in front of me.

"Thanks," I said, stirring the noodles mindlessly.

Sasha sat down across from me and nodded in Mitch's direction. "Anything?"

I shook my head. "He hasn't moved an inch."

"How are you doing?" Sasha asked, speaking delicately, as if her words were an unwieldy stack of fine china.

"I'm just numb. Like...this doesn't even seem real." I couldn't piece it all together. The circumstances were too coincidental. Or maybe that was how it felt when someone close to you died. "I keep thinking there has to be more to it. He drops everything, leaves in the middle of the night, and now he's dead? It's too weird."

Sasha stopped twirling her fork, and our eyes connected. "Life doesn't play fair. And death isn't ever something that feels well-timed or convenient. It always hits like a freight train."

I nodded, trying to decide how much I trusted her. She'd received the same call he did, but as her gaze stayed locked on mine, there was genuine sorrow in the way she looked at me. We'd cried together. She was grieving, too.

"How do I get my head around the fact that I'll never see my dad again?" Saying the words out loud made my throat sting and my eyes brim with tears.

"He loved you so much," she said, her shoulders slumping with sympathy. "It just poured out of him. He would talk about you constantly. So much that when you and I first met, I almost felt like I knew you already."

"Really?" I asked, pushing away my paranoia and taking the tiniest bite of my dinner. "I thought I was the family's dirty little secret."

"Not at all. I mean, I'd be lying if I said he didn't worry about you. But that man loved you kids like no one I've ever seen. He was so hard on the outside, but inside, his heart just overflowed. I think he told me every story there was about you, three or four times over."

"How serious were you guys?" I asked, drying the slow-crawling tears from my cheeks. "If you don't mind me asking."

"No, I..." Sasha finished her bite. "Very, I guess. I mean, there were certain obstacles that probably would have prevented us getting married, but..."

"Like what?"

"Ahhh...nothing I really want to get into. But I'll tell you this. He was the best man I've ever met. I know that's something people just sorta say...but I mean it. He was someone you could count on. And in this world, that's saying something."

"Trust me. I understand." I forced a smiled and looked back out at Mitch.

"He has to eat something," Sasha said after a moment. "Maybe I should go—"

"No." I got to my feet. "I'll go get him."

I headed through the sliding glass doors, across the backyard. As I entered the office, I paused to flip on the lights. To my surprise, they worked and filled the space with an offensive bright white. Mitch squinted but didn't look up. His blond hair stuck out in places from running his hands through it too many times, and his face was a red, blotchy mess. I finally exhaled and sat down beside him.

"You should come in. Sasha made dinner."

"It doesn't make sense."

I paused, feeling just as lost. "I know. It's so..."

"A whole life, gone. Like turning off a light switch." Mitch sat quietly for a moment, and finally looked me in the eyes. "It's not fair."

"It's..." I trailed off. I knew there was no resolution, no rationale I could come up with to make sense of it all. Nothing I could think of to help ease the pain or shock for either of us.

"We've got no parents," Mitch said. "What kids our age don't have parents? Think about the future, the next ten, twenty, thirty years? What does that even look like now? No parents at my high school graduation. No mother or father to come home from college to, to share holidays with, to meet my wife, your husband. Our kids will never know their grandparents. The rest of our lives are going to have this giant gaping hole."

"I know. I...know." I lowered my head as the ensuing silence enveloped us. Suddenly I felt completely inadequate. I was all he had left. The only one to comfort him. But how could I tell him everything would be okay when I knew it wouldn't? My nails dug into my palms.

Mitch suddenly turned to me. "I want to see his body."

I jolted at the break in silence. "I...already asked about that. Sasha told me that because of the current, they couldn't recover it."

Mitch got to his feet, suddenly manic and shaking. "I want to see Dad."

"I know, it's just—"

"I want to see him!" Mitch shouted, his lips taut with despair, eyes on fire.

I stood and started to approach him. "You can't."

As I reached out for him, he pulled away and punched the wall. It made a hole, but that wasn't enough. He reached for the sledgehammer and swung wildly, ripping through the drywall. Again, and again the emotion he'd been holding inside burst out of him. When he finally succumbed to fatigue, he slowly let the hammer slide from his grip.

I waited for the anger in the air to dissipate before putting a hand on Mitch's shoulder. He shrugged it off, continuing to stare at the holes he'd made.

"Come in and eat something..." I said, but Mitch wasn't listening. He was looking at something. A specific hole in the wall, narrowing his gaze as he approached it.

"What the..." He ignored my confused look and grabbed the hammer, knocking new holes every foot or so.

"Mitch," I yelled. "Stop already!"

"There's something here," he yelled back. "Look."

I finally saw it. A metal mechanism inside the wall. "What the heck is that?"

CHAPTER SIX

MITCH AND I FOLLOWED the metal gears and wiring until we found a small control panel in the wall. After taking a moment to study it, he reached in, tripped a lever and...*thunk*. A portion of the hardwood floor at the far end of the room popped up. I watched as Mitch walked over, found space for his fingers and yanked upward. The four-by-four section of the floor suddenly tilted back on hydraulics and revealed stairs.

Mitch turned to me. "This isn't on any blueprints I saw."

I pushed past him and slowly made my way down the stairs, listening for any sound in the darkness. Light from the office space spilled into the small underground cement bunker. As far as I could tell, it was twenty feet by twenty feet.

"Uhh, you didn't notice Dad building this?" I asked, squinting.

"No!" Mitch said, following me down. "He must have put it in when I was at the science competition..." Mitch's voice faded as I dropped off the last step.

A pressure plate turned everything on at once. Lights sprung to life amidst a cacophony of electric hums.

My lips parted in shock. "Whoa."

On the farthest wall, five flat retina screens flickered on, displaying things like satellite vistas, streaming intel, voice recognition and hacked camera views. Next to the setup sat a warren of bleeding-edge computer equipment. Thick bundled wires snaked in and around a stainless-steel supporting structure.

To the right of the stairs, a fully organized weapons arsenal was built into the wall. An assortment of sniper rifles topped with laser scopes were racked along the bottom. Several handguns sat above those. They were all fitted in black silhouette foam, which formed neat rows. A shelf on the left side held small bins which contained a myriad of grenades, both concussive and shrapnel, along with extra clips and boxes of bullets. Topping it off was a display of combat knives and several bulletproof vests.

Mitch's features twisted in confusion. "What is this place?"

"Looks like a Deep Cover Operations Center," I answered, trying to make sense of things.

"A deep what?" Mitch whispered, still staring.

I made my way to the weapons and reached for one of the handguns, pulling back the chamber to check if it was loaded. It was. I couldn't imagine Dad holding a gun, let alone knowing how to use one.

"A black ops room," I finally answered, setting the gun on a table most likely used for weapons prep. I nodded toward the screens. "That's intelligence data."

Mitch shook his head, clinging to the stairs like they were anchoring him to a different reality. "Dad made slides. For dishwashers!"

I was too lost in thought to respond. "I knew something was weird when they got that call..."

Mitch looked at me. "Why aren't you as freaked out as I am?"

"I am," I snapped. "This just makes more sense than flying to Beijing for an appliance crisis."

"But he takes business trips all the time..." Things seemed to click into place. "You think—"

"Stop asking me so many questions. Just let me think." I moved to a stainless-steel desk and tested one of the large drawers. It slid open. Inside, currency, passports, and cell phones were organized into neat piles.

I paused before I picked up a German passport. As I flipped it open, a well-groomed version of Dad stared back. My heart hurt at the sight of him. Who was he?

"Look at this," I said, waving Mitch over.

He grabbed the passport and stood in silence, shaking his head. But something else drew my attention: the dark brown envelope Dad had carried in from Sasha's car the night he left. I picked it up and noticed a big "S" written on the top.

Inside there was a silver flash drive and a small computer tablet. I instinctively slipped the flash drive into the tablet's port, but was immediately prompted for a password. After a few birthdays and anniversary dates it threatened to lock me out.

"Come here, Mr. MIT." I held out the tablet. "Can you unlock this?"

His lips were still pressed into a tight, stubborn line, but the challenge must have won him over because he took it, his brow low in concentration.

"Move over," he said.

I watched as he connected his cell to the computer tablet via Bluetooth. After finding something on his phone, he held down the volume + and power button at the same time. A picture of an Android bot appeared on screen followed by backend reboot options. He scrolled and typed with one hand on the flat screen, waited for system checks, and eventually reached out for the flash drive.

As soon as it was in, the tablet synched and a DECRYPTION SEQUENCE began. Mitch tapped the touch screen a few more times, typing in things I didn't understand until finally, the tablet's operating system was suddenly replaced with a single file. He tapped it and the folder opened.

Mitch stared at if for a second before handing it to me.

"What is it?" he asked.

I took the tablet and opened a few of the documents, scanning their contents. "I'm pretty sure...it's a mission dossier."

I glanced at Mitch and enlarged a photo, the full magnitude of the lie I'd been told sinking to the depths of my stomach like a bag of rocks. A picture of a forty-year-old man with a thick shock of prematurely white hair and a dark face riddled with pockmarks filled the screen.

"Who's he?"

I swiped a finger and read through what I could of the encrypted data. "If I had to guess, I'd say he's a target."

Mitch's voice spiked. "Target? Target for what?"

I swiped the screen again. "I dunno. I don't understand the verbiage or most of the symbols. Some of it is military, so I kinda get it, but you'd have to know the full code to really make sense of it. He's the target, that's all I can figure out."

As I paged through the electronic document, there was one more picture. I tapped and it enlarged.

The young man in the photo was in his early twenties at the most. He was handsome, with a prominent Adam's apple and thick black eyelashes surrounding clear green eyes. His dark, wavy hair fell against the tops of his bronze cheeks and whiskery jaw. Large exotic lips curved into a subtle smile revealing straight, white teeth.

"That guy a target, too?" Mitch asked.

"Um," I cleared my throat and read the photo details.

"He's the mission contact."

"What's that mean?"

I set the tablet on the desk and reached for my iPhone. "Someone local to help...with whatever it is you're there to do."

"Local where? Where did Dad go?"

I pointed to a set of coordinates below the contact picture: 23.1431° N, 82.3806° W

I whispered them out loud as I punched the numbers into the GPS on my phone. "It's a beach in Havana, Cuba."

Mitch's eyes went wide and he started to pace, trying to make sense of it all. "Is Dad an assassin, is he a killer?" He wiped his hands on his jeans and blew out deep sighs every few steps.

"I don't know—"

Mitch grew manic, talking louder and faster. "This target, that guy. Do you think Dad went there to kill him?"

Before I could answer, a voice echoed from the steps. "No. Those were not his orders. He was supposed to bring him in alive."

I turned to see Sasha as she stepped into the room. She collapsed the stairs back into the ceiling with a small handheld remote.

"Sasha?" Mitch stopped and stared at her.

"I'll need that drive and the tablet," she said, her demeanor cold and unfamiliar.

CHAPTER SEVEN

SASHA'S POSTURE WAS MUCH more rigid and her eyes hyper-focused. "The package should have been marked with an "S". I'm his liaison. He left that information for me."

"You're involved in this, too?" I asked. My eyebrows sank as I imagined Dad sneaking out to visit this room before leaving. It was all a charade. Deep down I knew he was trying to protect us, but the lie still felt like one of my nightmares.

"The tablet and the drive," Sasha repeated with a parental sternness.

With Dad missing, I didn't trust her. She was a liar, too. "And if I say no?"

"I care about you kids, and this is all very awkward. You were never supposed to know," Sasha said, revealing a gun in her hand. "That being said, please don't make me use this. Just give me the tablet and the drive."

I relented as she approached, extending the tablet out in front of me, but it wasn't in my nature to submit. My quieted rage had already grown into a glowing ember of red-hot anger. As Sasha took it, I trapped her gun hand and in one swift movement, twisted the weapon from her grip and shoved her back with force.

She recovered, gripping the tablet with one hand and straightening her shirt with the other. "Nicely done, but it doesn't change anything. I've already put in a call. There will be a tactical team here in minutes to clean up all this gear."

"Who's coming here? What team?" Mitch asked. I could almost see the quick beats of his pulse in the jumpy way he moved and the panicked look on his face.

Damn her for intruding in our lives. She had no right.

"Listen to me," Sasha continued, "this can all go really easy. They'll need to bring the two of you in. Just for a debrief and to sign some nondisclosure contracts. But if they see you waving a gun around—"

My forehead creased like a paper fan and I jabbed the gun at Sasha. "Then you'd better talk fast."

When Sasha didn't speak, Mitch stepped in front of her. "I treated you like family. I trusted you. The least you can do is tell us what's going on."

Sasha paused as if trying to reconcile what she was allowed to say versus what she'd like to say. She finally looked up at me. "Your father was an *Extractor*."

Mitch's gaze didn't waiver. "What is that?"

"There are criminals, all over the world, who are beyond the legal reach of our government. They've done horrible, atrocious things, but are untouchable because we can't secure extradition or it's too politically sensitive. Most of the time, our governmental agencies have to swallow the fact that these evil men get to live free."

"Except..." I said, leading Sasha. I gripped the gun firmly, but kept it comfortably at my side. Ready, in case she made a move.

"Except when the circumstances become too extreme and the government feels they must be captured at any cost."

"So we send someone to 'extract' them," I finished for Mitch's sake.

"Yes." Sasha nodded. "Someone off the books."

"So, Dad was what, then?" Mitch asked. "Some sort of international bounty hunter?"

"Like I said," Sasha answered, "an Extractor."

I'd heard rumors of people like that, but I never imagined my sense-talking, well-organized Dad could be one. I still couldn't picture it. If I hadn't seen the passports and the room, I'd be sure she was lying.

"That doesn't mean anything to me. Who did he work for specifically?" Mitch's voice rose with insistence. "The CIA?"

"No." Sasha hesitated, obviously not wanting to go

any further down this road. "The intelligence community is much different than it used to be. It's scattered, privatized. Sensitive ops are farmed out to help maintain deniability."

"She's saying Dad was a merc," I explained to Mitch. "A guy for hire." I turned to Sasha. "Which means *you're* no sales rep."

"Like I said, I'm just a liaison, a go-between." Sasha's posture softened. "Look, I realize all this is jarring. You must be feeling confused, betrayed—"

I cut her off. "Most of what's come out of your mouth has been a lie, so I'm gonna ask one last question and you better tell me the truth—Is my dad really dead?" As Sasha remained silent, I leveled the gun at her, my heart beating impatiently. "It's the only question that matters."

She lowered her head. "There's no way to know."

"How could you *not* know?" I yelled. Somewhere under the rush of anger there was a glimmer of hope, and I wouldn't let go of it. "How could you look me in the eyes and tell me he's dead and not be sure? Explain."

"Something went wrong and your father was captured, after that, all intel ceased."

"But..." Mitch stepped forward. "If you had to guess, do you think he's really dead?"

Sasha's large, pouty lips and dimpled cheeks turned down with sympathy. "I don't think so. Not yet."

"There's a chance he'll be rescued?" Mitch asked, his eyes lighting up.

She shook her head. "You don't understand. Harry was never there. This op never existed."

Mitch's shoulders sank. "What are you saying?"

"I'm saying...your father's been officially *disavowed*."

"So, they're just gonna leave him there to rot," I snapped as I began absent-mindedly tapping my thumb against the pistol grip. I could feel myself start to lose control of my emotions. There wasn't time to talk this out. I needed to *do* something.

"Truth is..." Sasha said, struggling to finish. "They don't keep men like Harry prisoner for long. Even if the higher-ups wanted to make a play at a rescue, the team they sent in probably wouldn't get to him in time."

With a quick thrust, I slammed Sasha against the wall and pressed the gun into her stomach. "You're gonna give me details. Everything you know. Now."

"No. I'm not." Sasha's gaze hardened as she stared me in the eyes. "I loved your father. I told you that and I meant it. It's the only reason I've compromised the information I have. But this talk is officially over." She raised her eyebrows. "So I guess you're just going to have to shoot."

I clenched my teeth, lowering the gun and backing away. Time was on her side, not mine.

Mitch began to pace again. "This isn't happening."

"I'm so sorry," Sasha said with genuine regret in her voice.

I turned to Sasha. "Do what you gotta do. Burn this place to the ground for all I care. But me and my brother are not hanging around to be interrogated."

Sure, the military worked under a set of laws and government policies, but private companies had their own moral code, one I couldn't trust. To them, Mitch and I were just loose ends that needed tying up.

My pulse quickened as I pointed the gun at Sasha again, realizing this time I might actually have to use it.

She gave me a look. "Tara..."

"Open the hatch," I said in a strong, even tone.

After a moment, Sasha reached into her pocket and clicked the handheld remote to lower the staircase. Cool night air rushed in from above as it locked into place. I grabbed Mitch by the arm and kept my eyes on Sasha as I headed for the exit, but she didn't try to stop us. Once we reached the backyard, Mitch yanked himself free.

"Let go of me."

"You want to stick around?" I asked, hiding the gun in the back of my shorts.

Mitch held his arms out wide. "I don't know."

Suddenly, pulling up to the front of the house were five black, nondescript vehicles. I grabbed his arm again. "Fine. But do me a favor and keep moving while you decide."

I led him behind the office building, to an old, loose plank of fence I'd used in high school to sneak out. Low voices hummed in the distance as we crept through our neighbor's backyard, slinking along the edge of their blue pool, glowing in the night, and onto a parallel street.

"Keep against the fence. In the shadows," I whispered to Mitch as I glided along every parked car and tested locks until one finally opened. A 1980s dark green Ford Taurus. Looking over my shoulder I slid inside, ducking under the steering column to find the wire bundle. The nostalgic rush of deciphering the ignition and battery cables from a tangled nest felt like an unsettled hive of bees in my chest. As the engine fired up, I let out a held breath and hid the gun in the glove box.

I popped the passenger side door open and locked eyes with Mitch. "Get in."

He did, thank God, and I gunned the car away. A few blocks from the house, I headed onto the freeway. After driving a few miles in silence, I realized we had nowhere to go. We'd probably have to sleep in the car tonight. I bit my lip thinking through different options.

"This is crazy," Mitch finally spoke. He stared out the windshield, his arms crossed. "I can't believe Dad lied to us." He turned to me. "Why are you not more freaked out?"

My eyes widened. "Who said I'm not?"

"You don't look freaked out."

"What do you want me to do, scream? Pound the dash?"

"Yeah," his voice spiked. "For starters."

"I'm just trying to focus on what I can control. I need to think."

Mitch stared at me for another few moments. "What

are we even doing? Pull over. Right now!"

I swerved onto the shoulder and skidded to a stop. "What?" I yelled. "What?!"

"Why are we running?" Mitch dragged both hands through his hair. "We didn't do anything."

"Because I don't have time to be detained, debriefed, or whatever else they have planned for us." I watched the taillights of other cars speed by and blur into a red glow up ahead.

"Needing time implies you have a plan."

I let out a deep breath. No matter how many plans ran through my head, there was only one real option for getting Dad back if he was alive. "I'm going to Cuba."

"Say again?"

Saying it out loud only solidified my decision. I couldn't live with giving up. Not if there was even the tiniest chance. "I have the coordinates of Dad's local contact. I'm gonna go find the guy."

"And then what?" Mitch asked, leaning forward to look me in the eyes.

"I don't know, I have no freakin' idea. Okay?" I shouted. "Find out what happened, I guess. Maybe find out where Dad is. See if there's any way..."

"To what? Save him? You're just one person."

I combed my loose bangs back over my head, stress knotting up my tight shoulders. "I don't know what I'm supposed to do. All I know is what I can do. What I feel like I should do. At least it's a starting point."

"I get that, I do. But starting point for what?" Mitch asked as a semitruck barreled by and shook the car. "You have no idea what you're getting into."

"You're right. But I know what disavowed means. It means no one's going to help Dad. Ever. I also know there's only one reason guys take time before killing someone. If he's alive, they're gonna torture him. They're going to bleed whatever info they can get out of him...then they're gonna kill him," I said, gripping the steering wheel so tightly the blood receded from my knuckles. "So, yeah, this is probably another of my long string of horribly bad ideas. But I'm still going. I can't sit here and do nothing."

Mitch stayed quiet.

"Where can I drop you off?" I asked.

He tapped his fingers against his shorts and finally turned to answer. "If you're going, I'm going with you."

"No." I shook my head. "You're getting lost somewhere."

"Let's not start playing the protective big sister all of a sudden."

"I'm not protecting you," I answered honestly. "I just can't have you getting in my way. You're not built for this. I love you, but you'd only hold me back."

"Yeah?" The nostrils of his sharp-edged nose flared in anger. "Well, if this is about getting down there and figuring stuff out, I'd say I'm exactly built for this. One of us in this car is in Mensa, and the other can't spell it."

I stared at him, but didn't answer, not because I

agreed with him, but because another thought surfaced as he was ranting. The idea of leaving him behind for Sasha's men to find and do who-knows-what to was the only thing that tipped the scale in his favor.

"Trust me," Mitch continued, "the last thing I want to do is spend any more time with you than I have to. If this was any other scenario, I'd bail on you in a second. That's what we do in this family, right?" Mitch held my gaze for a beat before continuing. "But if I can add a few percentage points to whatever chance there is to save Dad's life...I'm going."

I thought for a moment, trying to calm down. "Fine."

"Okay, so...," Mitch nodded, thinking. "...what about Sasha? What if they're waiting for us at the airport?"

"We're not going to the airport." I laughed. "You don't just fly to Cuba."

"Right, of course. So...how are we getting there?"

"Put your seat belt on," I said, looking over my shoulder as I reentered the freeway. "We've got a bit of a drive ahead."

"Drive? To where?"

I set my eyes on the road ahead. "The Keys."

CHAPTER EIGHT

I DROVE ALL NIGHT. By the time I finally steered the car through the narrow, stick-straight streets of Key West, my eyelids hung like heavy curtains ready to close. Mitch slept most of the dull ride, crashing hard after taking down two drive-thru cheeseburgers, which gave me more time to think. That was both a good thing and a bad thing. I was able to come up with a hypothetical plan, but once that was in place, there wasn't much left to do but tear myself apart.

The moment they'd gotten those calls I knew something wasn't right, and still, I'd let him go. If I would have insisted he tell me the truth, maybe I could have gone with him. At the very least I should have followed. A dozen different "what-ifs" tortured me as I drove, but none of them mattered. The reality was one of two things:

he was either being tortured for information or he was already dead.

As I conjured nightmarish visuals, my foot sank into the gas petal. My chest felt like it might cave in.

Just focus on the plan, I told myself, trying to relax my shoulders.

I was pretty sure I could get us to Cuba. It was only ninety miles from the tip of Key West. If families coming in this direction could make it on a raft, I could pull it off going the other way with the right kind of boat. The biggest problem would be the Cuban patrols. While they were set up to keep people from getting out, not in, they were known to shoot first and ask questions later.

I glanced at Mitch as he began to stir and looked away when he sat up. Having him with me was going to make this a lot harder, but I had to admit it was comforting to not be completely alone. He was the only one who knew how desperate I was, who understood why I *had* to do this.

As I turned down Sunset Key Drive, Mitch ogled the houses lining the streets. They were enormous and beyond opulent. Their towering facades and manicured front yards sparkled with accent lighting that gleamed like gold in the night. He rubbed his eyes with the palms of his hands.

"Where are we?" he asked.

"Key West," I answered.

"Yeah, I know that, but why are we in this specific area? Do you know someone around here?"

I didn't answer. Mitch was on board in theory, but chances were he wasn't going to like my plan. I slowed the car a bit as I glided through the exclusive neighborhood. According to Google, this street was supposed to hold the most expensive houses in Key West. Five, ten, sometimes fifteen million dollars each. They were all nauseatingly lavish and well groomed, with yards that backed right into the water. Quarter-million-dollar cars sat in the driveways, which meant million-dollar boats in back. Some would be large boats, but most would be very, very fast. Because there was nothing a tubby, balding, middle aged rich businessman loved more than going fast.

Mitch started fidgeting with the old-school window crank, endlessly spinning the knob until I gave him a look.

"Did you know Key West was originally called Cayo Hueso or 'Island of Bones'?" he finally blurted out.

I kept my focus on the houses as I drove. "No."

"It was a Spanish settlement early on, but when Key West's first white settlers arrived, they found it littered with skeletons. Either from a battle or maybe a Calusa Indian burial ground."

"That's fascinating, Mr. Wikipedia, but I'm trying to concentrate. Help me look for a house with side gates."

"Side gates? Why?"

Just as he asked, I found one and parked under a thick sea grape tree. As I reached over Mitch to grab the gun out of the glove box, his eyes locked onto it.

"Are we really going to need that?"

"Mitch," I said, letting out an exasperated puff of air, "we're not picking him up from the airport."

He shook his head as if acknowledging the stupid question. "I know, I know."

"If you want to back out, this is the time."

He shook his head again, and we both stepped out of the car.

"Are—" he started, but I silenced him with a finger to my lips, and tucked the gun into the back of my shorts.

Waving him forward, I darted between two enormous houses. As expected, the side gate to the one I had zeroed in on was open. It was something I'd learned in my breaking-and-entering days—people always forgot to lock their gates. I headed toward the backyard and Mitch trailed behind. There were no lights on in either house, which was typical. These enormous, beautiful houses sat empty for ten months out of the year. The thought of it made me sick. During my time in Iraq, I'd seen people starving, barely existing in squalor. I wondered how the uber-rich lived with themselves.

I'd read a book in the juvie library once that said nearly half of the Forbes four hundred richest Americans inherited the majority of their wealth. And less than twenty percent started out as upper-middle class or worse. To me that meant a whole lot of rich people born on third base, thinking they hit a triple. Which only made what I was about to do that much easier.

With the coast clear, I led Mitch across the spacious

backyard, past a giant infinity pool and down to the dock. There, up on a mechanical lift, sat a brand-new 28-foot Outerlimits go-fast boat. I walked up close and looked it over, running a hand across its hull and barely refraining from giving an appreciative whistle.

Besides boosting cars, I'd done a little boat work on the side. Not much, but enough to know my away around watercraft. This boat had a 5-stepped deep-V bottom, light carbon fiber deck, and epoxy e-glass hull with a high-performance Mercury motor, capable of 1300 hp. All in all, it was built for speed and exactly what I was looking for.

My cheeks lifted into a grin. "This'll do."

Mitch looked around nervously. "We're just gonna steal this guy's boat?"

"More like borrow."

"We're just gonna *borrow* his boat?"

I shrugged. "If he doesn't get it back, his insurance will cover it."

Along the edge of the dock, I found a small white, cylindrical control panel. I lifted the lid and pressed the button to lower the boat into the water, but nothing happened.

"What makes you think it's a guy?" I asked, squinting at the panel.

"Quit screwing around, you know what I mean."

I pressed the lift button again, but it still didn't work. Resisting the urge to kick the cylinder, I tried the other buttons.

"Like I said, this is as good a time as any for you to back out. Chances are, we're gonna be doing a lot worse things than this, and the last thing I need is you questioning my every move. So, if any of this upsets your delicate sensibilities, the car's right out there."

Mitch stood there for a beat, and I silently hoped he'd listen as I tried to mash the lift button one more time. It was finally dawning on me that he could actually get hurt. Not to mention, his entire future, everything he'd worked for, could be hanging in the balance. Even if I could keep him safe in Cuba, we were about to enter a foreign country illegally. That had to be frowned upon by the deans at MIT, and that was just for starters. Although running back home to Sasha didn't exactly feel like a full-proof plan either. I opened my mouth to revisit the options, but he stepped up and slapped my hand away.

"What the hell?" I snapped at him.

He walked to the other side of the dock to a circuit breaker, popped it open and flicked it on.

"Helps to have electricity."

I held back a smile, and then hit the lift button. Maybe it *would* be good to have him along. With a mechanical whirl, the go-fast boat immediately descended, splashing gently into the water.

I nodded to Mitch. "Get me something to pry open the ignition box."

After looking around, Mitch came back with a rock

the size of a cantaloupe. "This is all I could find."

I hopped into the boat and smashed the ignition box, but as the bundle of wires fell out, lights flickered on inside the house.

"Ummm, I'd get in the boat if I were you," I called down to Mitch.

"There's someone home," he gasped as more lights came on. The back door scissored open. "Someone's coming."

"Like I said, get in the boat!" My hands worked, pulling and twisting. Finally, a spark arced between wires and, as the giant motor rumbled to life, I turned to see a bald, pasty white man charging toward them. His robe slipped opened as he ran, his enormous belly flopping up and down.

"Hey! That's my boat!" the man screamed as he fumbled to put on glasses.

"Time to go," I said. Mitch hopped in, and I backed the boat clear of the lift just as the man made it to the dock. I jammed the throttle, launching us forward. With the wheel pinned, the boat fishtailed around, unleashing a giant wake that drenched the man and knocked him onto his butt.

THANKFULLY, IT WAS a calm night. I piloted the go-fast over glassy water that reflected the moon like a spilled puddle of liquid mercury. With the nose of the boat angled perpetually in the air, I rocketed toward Cuba without looking back. The only thing that mattered was moving forward. Wind slammed against my face, chilling my cheeks, my dark hair lifting and swirling behind me. I narrowed my eyes, trying to decipher the direction of the wind so as to compensate for any drift, and kept a firm grip on the wheel. If I continued south, there would be no missing the curved hip of land that hugged the Florida Keys.

As soon as I was on my way, the gravity of what I was doing set in. There was no military to back me up. I was going in alone, unprepared, and ill-equipped. But I couldn't let that sway me. I'd trained for situations far more dangerous than this. I'd been on missions I didn't think I'd live through, felt bullets rip through flesh, and looked dead men in the eyes.

Still, no matter how determined I felt, fear rose in my stomach like a flock of birds bursting into flight. This was different. Dad's life was on the line. And I had Mitch to watch out for, which was its own knot of worry sitting tight in my chest.

In just over an hour, the distant rim of Cuba's expansive coastline became clear. I kept the boat full throttle and took in the view. Something about it seemed unearthly. Stars gleamed against night's blackened canvas, and the subtle light that streamed through the shore fog turned the horizon into an impressionistic painting. I glanced at Mitch pressed against his seat, a white-knuckled death grip on the handrail. His eyes pinched as the wind buffeted them nearly shut. He looked so young, and I immediately felt guilty. He shouldn't have come.

I turned my focus back to the water. *Just stick with the plan and run through the steps,* I told myself. *One at a time.* I would treat this, and Mitch, like any other operation. Get in. Get the job done. Get out. It was the only way to keep a clear head.

I steered the boat for another twenty minutes before I spotted the Cuban patrol boats. Seeing their lights sweep across the water was gut-sinking, but I'd expected them. Keeping the motor running, I glided to a stop.

"Why are we stopping?" Mitch asked, blinking moisture back into his eyes as he stared out at the now prominent coast of Cuba.

"See those spotlights in the distance?" I said, pointing to the right. There were several dots of light headed toward us. "That's a Cuban military patrol."

Mitch shot to his feet. "What?"

"I thought we might get lucky and avoid them, but we must've been spotted."

"Which means?" he asked.

I stood and found the glove box near the passenger seat. "I've got a plan...but the owner of this boat's not gonna like it much," I said, rummaging through the storage compartment.

The Cuban military were still about a mile away, which meant we had at least another minute before we were in range of their weapons, even if they had a fifty-caliber machine gun onboard. I knew from countless hours in weapons courses that at two thousand yards, the accuracy of those guns dropped off dramatically. Which meant we were safe for now, but not for much longer.

"And the plan is...?" Mitch asked, squinting.

I held out a wet-bag, pulled the gun from the back of my shorts and dropped it inside. "We're getting off. Put your cell phone and wallet in here. It's waterproof."

Mitch watched like a frightened puppy as I turned the boat at an angle, back out to sea. Using some loose docking rope, I tied the steering wheel into a locked position and throttled forward. It was an instant, easy, makeshift autopilot.

"What?" Mitch spun and looked out at the coast. "How far are we from shore?" he yelled over the sudden tear of the engine.

"'Bout a mile and a half," I yelled back, leaving the wheel and pulling Mitch over to the side.

"We're jumping? Wait, wait."

"What?" my voice carried through the wind.

Mitch's hair tossed around wildly as he thought about it. "Are there sharks?"

"Probably. Look, every second you don't jump, the swim gets longer." I motioned to the open sea. The boat was moving fast and diagonally away from the coast.

Mitch's face flushed with fear, his tall, lean body jumpy with adrenaline, but he didn't argue further. He simply turned, put one foot on the edge of the boat, and leapt. Without thought, I took a breath and dove in immediately after, my body skipping across the cold water like a stone at 30 mph. The force of the impact felt like being thrown from a moving car and drowning at the same time, but I gripped the wet-bag like it was my only lifeline. I must have bounced a good fifty yards before finally spraying to a stop.

Coughing and spitting water, I let out a hacking cough as Mitch surfaced beside me. He choked and groaned, but the plan had worked. The go-fast sped away, and after a few moments, the three Cuban patrol turned to chase the empty boat.

"I think I just got my first enema," Mitch said, still coughing.

"Gross."

"I'm serious, I—whoa!" Mitch jerked. "I'm pretty sure something big just bumped me!"

I swam over. "Stay close, focus on the shoreline. Nice, even strokes."

Mitch looked back at the boat, but I grabbed his chin, pointing it forward.

"Just swim, and don't stop."

CHAPTER NINE

EARLY MORNING SUN FORCED its way through the fronds of a giant palm, casting striped shadows across Mitch's face as he slept below. In my groggy state I imagined we were in the Bahamas. I glanced around, hardly remembering how I'd gotten to this small, secluded beach after last night's swim. Then I remembered Dad.

I closed my eyes, trying to hide from the hollow ache in my gut. We'd made it, but I still didn't feel any closer to saving him.

One step at a time, I reminded myself.

As I squinted out over the bright sand, I noticed the "neumáticos," about a hundred yards off shore. Growing up in Florida, I'd heard about them, the Cuban locals who fished from inner tubes. With a fishing net spread over the tube, like a hammock, they'd float around the current and lazily try to catch lunch.

I slid myself into a sitting position, shading my eyes with my hand. The sun blazed so hot it reduced shadows to mere spots of ink, and the ocean air carried the scent of magnolias as foamy waves tumbled onto the quiet beach. But I didn't have time to enjoy the view.

I nudged Mitch in the side. After a couple of loud moans, he finally propped himself on his elbows and scanned the sunlit sand with nervous eyes.

"You okay?" I asked, removing my tennies and peeling off sand-caked socks. I shook them clean, then quickly put them back on.

"Yeah," Mitch mumbled, doing the same.

The wet-bag from the boat sat half-buried at my side. I opened it, grabbed the gun, and racked the chamber several times, checking that it was dry and free of grit.

"Come on," I said, getting to my feet. I tucked the gun into the back of my shorts and tossed Mitch his wallet and phone. "Got to keep moving."

"Wait," Mitch stopped me. "Shouldn't we ditch this?" He held up his cell. "What if they trace it? Follow us here?"

I sputtered out a laugh and looked back at him. "Don't count on it. If they were willing to get their hands dirty and come to Cuba, they wouldn't need people like Dad. And even if they did come...let 'em. We need all the backup we can get."

I brushed off my shorts as best I could, and ambled onto the main street with Mitch close behind. As I hit a large crosswalk, I finally got a look at the city of Havana. It was a living, breathing dichotomy, partially frozen in the past with horse-drawn carriages and crumbling colonial buildings. Yet, at the same time, a modern marvel with art deco architecture that rivaled Los Angeles and New York.

I paused, thinking through the next part of my plan. We needed cash and possibly a vehicle. I looked around, trying to decipher which direction would lead me to a slum, and then motioned to Mitch. "This way."

Within the next few blocks, the scenery grew shockingly seedy. I took a hard right and headed down a pothole-strewn street. The surroundings in this part of town looked more like war-torn Beirut with burnt cars and heaps of trash collected in corners. An entire meal—box, plastic fork, cup—sat on a curb, abandoned by the eater.

We passed a pair of drugged-out men who sat on the curb and stared out at the traffic, each of them transfixed as if watching TV. Their yellowed, blood-shot eyes followed us as we turned another corner.

The heat was thick and heavy. My whole body suddenly felt wet. I shook my shirt and wiped a stream of sweat off my forehead. It dripped onto the parched street dust before instantly evaporating.

"How's your Spanish?" I asked Mitch.

"Took three years, two of them were AP."

"Good." I nodded. "Most people speak English here, but we might need it at some point."

We passed a long row of broken-down, three-story

stone town houses, transformed at some point by the Revolution into a colorful backdrop of ruin and decay. Large, marble colonnades were refaced with whatever color was available—green, red, bright yellow. It was a beautiful, yet tragic kaleidoscope.

A small bus station sat to our right. It was a run-down sad affair, like most of the nearby structures. The terminal was surrounded by a bundle of ramshackle booths fashioned from tarps and cast-off wood, a foul tent city with vendors pushing questionable food and second-hand clothing. An ancient Greyhound bus staggered into the lumpy parking lot, its tired air brakes hissed in protest as it stopped and disgorged a few elderly passengers, but none of them matched the personality type I was looking for. I needed someone who carried lots of cash, which meant we had to look someplace more secluded.

The bus's rusting, graffiti-covered shell shuddered in time with the engine, and after its doors squeaked shut, it rolled on down the road.

Up ahead I spotted an open weed-choked lot full of decaying junk and started in that direction.

"What are we doing here? Shouldn't we be heading to the coordinates?" Mitch asked, his head on a swivel. "I thought we were going to try and find Dad's contact."

"We are."

The lot was scattered with bundles of randomly strung wire, bald tires in ditches, and old refrigerators that lay dead on their backs. On the other side stood a row of apartments with yellowed cloth curtains that billowed from windows. On each balcony old men chewed on blunt cigars, comatose in canvas chairs. Their tan bellies winked from open shirts and their beer cans sparkled in the sun.

"The coordinates are at the beach, not this dump."

"We need to pick up a few things first," I said, my eyes scanning the alleyways for lone, sketchy-looking men.

"*Things?* Could you be a little more specific?"

I glanced back at Mitch, knowing he'd completely flip over my plan.

"No."

Before he could respond, I pulled him behind a row of rusting metal barrels and ducked into a crouching position.

"Stay here," I said, pulling the gun from the back of my shorts.

I peered between the barrels and caught sight of the guy I had my eye on. Hopefully, he'd had a good day. I checked the clip for bullets and slammed it back in, then chambered a round. The click and snap of the gun got Mitch's attention.

"Wait," he stopped me. "Why do you need that?"

"Look, I can't have you questioning everything I'm doing. I'm here to get Dad, no matter what it takes. Trust me, or go find a hotel and let me do my thing."

Mitch's nervous eyes danced back and forth between me and the gun.

I sighed heavily and wiped my damp forehead. If this

were any other operation I'd include him, we'd discuss a plan. "Fine." I nodded toward the shady-looking man a block ahead. "One block up, left side. See that guy? He's a dealer, probably meth."

"Uh-huh."

"We might have to bribe Dad's contact, and dealers have cash."

"So, what? You're going to rob him?" Mitch scoffed, laughing at the absurd idea.

I didn't smile. "That sweet, kindly drug dealer? Uh, yeah." I tucked the gun back into my shorts. "He's gonna take me into that alley. I'll ask to buy whatever he's selling—"

"Hold on—"

"If I'm not back in ten minutes..." I shook my head. "I'll be back."

I took off before Mitch could say anything else. As I got closer, I could make the man out more clearly. He was tall with a shaved head and the shiny coating of someone on too many pills. The dealer finished a cigarette in one aggressive pull, stomped it out and leaned against a wall with a faded mural of a skeleton dressed like Uncle Sam, holding a knife. Under it read: "No Imperialismo."

I slowed as I approached, and the tall man nodded, lifting an eyebrow.

"Do you speak English?" I asked.

The dealer smiled, revealing a mouth full of chipped, stained teeth. "Of course, beautiful girl."

Five years ago, a guy like this would have made me nervous, but carrying a gun and knowing how to use it builds confidence.

"Uh, what do you have?" I asked, acting naïve and tucking my hair behind my ear.

"Anythin' you need." The dealer's pupils jittered back and forth like he was following a hummingbird. "Not here. Police. Follow me."

"Okay." I kept my eyes wide and innocent, trying to seem unsure. "Just not too far."

The dealer led me down a trash-strewn alley. He finally stopped and pulled out a tiny bag with a tinfoil ball inside. "Bueno rock, eh?"

I reached for the bag but the dealer pulled it away. As his arm lifted, I saw the black handle of a gun hidden under his coat.

"That's fifty, American dollars...but hay otro ways if no money."

He moved closer and ran a rough hand with dirty fingernails down my bare arm.

God, I wanted to punch him in the face so badly, but his gun meant I had to be more careful. The dealer moved in, his stained teeth and old-sock smell made me want to gag. I pulled away, and his lip curled into an angry snarl. Screw it, I thought. My fist connected with his nose in a quick pop.

"Puta Madre!" he shouted.

Blood gushed from his nostrils, and he instinctively

covered his face with his hands. My opportunity. I reached behind my back for the gun, but someone else caught my arm before I lifted my shirt.

"Estas loca, pretty girl?" the other man breathed as he wrapped my neck in a chokehold.

I pressed my chin into the thick crook of his elbow and struggled to break free. The dealer's friend was big, but a quick heel to the nuts and an elbow in the gut...

It was a good plan, until I had a Glock pointed at my head.

The dealer's eyebrow twitched and he ground his teeth back and forth. "You wanna play, little mama?" He dragged the tip of his gun along the side of my cheek, wiping blood from his lips.

Just as I was about to spit in his face, the dealer's head suddenly jerked sideways like someone had removed his spine. He dropped to the ground in a crumpled heap, leaving Mitch standing behind him with a brick in his hand.

The surprise was enough of a distraction that I was finally able to heel-kick my attacker in the balls, slide the dealer's gun away with my foot, and draw my own from the waist of my shorts.

"I thought I told you to stay put," I scolded Mitch as I held the big guy at gun point.

Mitch kept his eyes on the knocked-out drug dealer. "Or, how about '*thanks for saving my life*'?"

"Hey! You," I ignored Mitch and focused on the

dealer's friend. "Money and keys."

For the first time, I got a good look at the guy's face. He wasn't as strong as he was fat. His entire demeanor changed now that the gun was on him, his brown eyes were large with fear and the rest of his face sagged like a pouting bulldog.

He stared back at me and shook his head over and over.

"Oh, don't pretend like you don't know what I'm saying. Keeeys! Moooneeey!"

"Tus llaves y dinero," Mitch translated.

While the fat man dug in his pockets, pulling out loose change, I rifled through the dealer's, finding a roll of money wrapped in a rubber band and a set of car keys with a Cadillac emblem on the chain.

"Ask him where the car is," I said to Mitch as I snatched up the extra gun and stuck it in my shorts.

"Dónde está el carro? Qué color es?" Mitch asked.

I dangled the keys at the fat man.

He pointed, his voice whiney with panic. "En la calle de allá. El azul."

"Got it?" I asked Mitch, keeping my gun trained on the two Cubans.

He nodded. "Let's go."

I walked the first few paces backwards, just to be sure they wouldn't try to follow us.

"Son of a..." Mitch said, rubbing his face once we were far enough away. "That was intense."

"I told you. I'm gonna do my thing," I said, looking over my shoulder. Luckily, there was no sign of the men. "If you can't handle it, get a hotel."

Mitch followed quick at my heels. "Can't handle it? I saved your life!"

"I was fine," I said, secretly a little embarrassed that my nerd-boy baby brother had come to my rescue. "But thank you." Chances were, I'd have gotten myself out of the situation, but I had to admit, it was nice to have back-up.

"You're welcome." He nodded, a smug grin creeping into his cheeks.

I rolled my eyes at him. "Don't get cocky."

The two of us walked in silence, scanning the street for a blue Cadillac to match the keys. Sure enough, the whiney bulldog was telling the truth. I stopped next to a classic '55, tried the key, and *pop*. The door unlocked. Hiding the second gun against my leg I looked back one last time. "Get in."

Mitch obeyed without question and I fired up the car, hiding both guns under the old gray bench seat. It was ripped and worn down to the yellow foam stuffing, but the body of the vehicle was what mattered. It was the perfect camouflage. As I drove forward, it completely blended in with the other "Yank tanks" that roamed the streets.

The classic American autos seemed to be what most of the locals drove in Cuba. I remembered Vince telling me about how back in the sixties, the U.S. started an embargo against Cuba, cutting trade between the two countries. So almost all the cars around here were classics. I watched as a line of Yank tanks passed in front of us like an antique car parade.

"Got your phone?" I asked Mitch as I piloted down a large, traffic-choked road. The roads here were in horrible shape, cracked and pitted. The mere act of driving felt like rearranging my skeleton.

He nodded, pulling out his iPhone. "Where are we going?" he asked.

"To the beach," I answered. "You wanted to go to the beach, right? Do you remember the coordinates of Dad's contact?"

"Does E equal MC squared?"

I laughed. "Careful, your nerd brain is showing."

"Shut up."

Mitch placed the phone on the dash and I followed the navigation, my heart beating faster. The dealer holdup was necessary, but we were running out of time. I pressed harder on the accelerator, urging the car in front of me to speed up.

"You know," Mitch said, leaning back. "You really do owe me one."

I held back my smile. I'd never hear the end of *the one time Mitch saved my life*. "I told you. I had it—"

"Wait," he interrupted. "Shouldn't I have one of the guns?"

"Just slow down, Mr. Calculus. Just because you hit a

guy with a brick doesn't mean I trust you with a gun."

"What if we run into trouble again?" he argued.

I imagined Mitch with a weapon, fumbling with it and accidentally shooting me in the leg.

"Practice making mean faces?"

CHAPTER TEN

THE COAST OF CUBA was an endorphin-releasing dreamscape. Clear water and sandy beaches provided an oasis for flocks of tan, beautiful locals. Flashes of coffee-colored skin, strong white teeth and long, smooth legs blurred past. A stark contrast to the rotting barrios we'd just left, everything here was shiny and new. Vendor stands lined the entire strand. Some peddled food and drink; others sold activities such as guided snorkeling, base-jumping, zip lines, and parasailing.

I clutched Mitch's cell phone in my hand, following the beacon to the exact destination. "This is the location of the coordinates, but GPS on cell phones aren't exact. I'd say we're looking at a radius of a few hundred yards give or take. Do you remember what the contact looked like?" I asked, recalling the image of a handsome face with dark eyelashes and large lips.

Mitch nodded. "Yeah. Young and tan. Pretty much like every guy on the beach here."

I waved an arm at the line of vendors. "He should be in one of these huts. Ideally, you want to meet your contact at a stationary location."

"There's a lot of beach and a ton of huts. Should we split up?"

I hesitated. We weren't in any imminent danger, but still, the idea of letting Mitch out of my sight made me nervous.

"We could scan the beach in half the time," he added.

"Okay," I agreed, handing back his phone. "Call me if you spot him. And be careful."

As Mitch headed in the opposite direction, I fanned the back of my neck with my hand. The heat and humidity made it feel like I was walking underwater. I looked down. Although I could use a change of clothes, I appreciated the fact that I wasn't in full military gear while slugging through this particular stretch of hot sand. Thankfully, I was still wearing the cut-off jean shorts I'd slipped on yesterday at the house. The memory of painting the office felt like so long ago.

Dad's only been missing for one day, two at the most, I reminded myself. *Please be alive.*

Sweat began to soak through the front of my shirt as I searched the beach. I flipped the bottom of my tank top up, then down through the neckline and pulled it tight.

Feeling a little cooler, I continued down the coast, my eyes ticking along every vendor shack. After my second pass to the end of the line and back, I spotted him. The contact from Dad's digital dossier stood beneath the grassy roof right in front of me.

I sat down on someone's empty beach chair and decided to watch him for a moment. He was clean shaven, but his hair still hung around his cheeks like it did in the picture. He was striking up close, his skin shockingly smooth and the color so evenly tan it almost glowed. Instant annoyance washed over me. In my experience, overly attractive guys were either jerks or idiots. Or both. And I didn't have time to deal with either.

I scanned the beach for Mitch, but didn't see him. As I looked back, I noticed Dad's contact staring. Immediately I turned away. *Could he possibly recognize me*?

That didn't make sense. Dad would never have compromised us.

I looked back, just to be sure.

He smiled and gave me a slight nod, but I didn't see any recognition in his eyes. He probably just saw a lost girl alone on the beach. Easy target. Guys like him were always trying to get laid.

I reached for my cell, ready to get this over with. After several rings, the sound of Mitch's voice came as an instant relief.

"I found him," I said. "About two hundred yards west of where we started. I'll wait 'til you get here."

I leaned back in the beach chair as I waited, letting the sun work its magic on my pale arms and legs. My eyes drifted to the water, but I was acutely aware of everything happening in and around the hut. I managed to catch his name, Andy, as a few teenage girls wandered by and giggled something to him in Spanish.

The stand where he worked sold excursions. From what I could tell, they were essentially guided packages such as scuba tours, zip line outings, and the like. As I waited, the two of us exchanged a couple of glances, and I decided it wouldn't hurt to shoot him a smile. Flirtation might be a good angle to get him alone.

Just as I was about to give up on waiting for Mitch and head over, a local scumbag with a grown-out Mohawk and copious tattoos slid in front of the excursion shack.

I took mental notes as Andy referred to the man as 'Jorge.' Pretending to lose interest, I subtly watched the conversation play out. It turned instantly aggressive.

I couldn't understand what they were saying, but it was clear Jorge was threatening Andy who tried desperately to defuse the situation. Jorge grabbed him and shoved him against the back wall of the shack, and I reflexively jerked forward, but stopped myself. Jorge jabbed his finger at Andy, unloaded a few more threats and finally stormed off.

"Hey," Mitch said, stepping beside me. He looked over at Andy. "You're right, that's the guy in the picture."

"Let's go talk to him," I said, getting to my feet.

As I trudged through the hot, thick sand and slid up against the worn wooden shack, I amped up my flirtatious smile. I needed information, and this guy was going to give it to me.

When he saw me, he offered a wide grin, which faded slightly when his eyes found Mitch.

"Hola. Qué bolá?"

"Hi," I said, with an overly-sweet inflection. "Do you speak English?"

"Very well, I think." His voice was a deep hum. "My name is Andy, and yours?"

"Tara," I answered, waiting to see if my name would jog any memory.

It didn't seem to.

"Beautiful. So, what excursions are you interested in?"

"You know, I'm not sure," I said, faking interest. "Maybe you could help a girl out?"

"Is this for you and your boyfriend?" Andy asked, nodding toward Mitch who stood a few paces behind.

I looked back and frowned. "Him?"

"Me?" Mitch laughed.

I turned to Andy. "That's my little brother."

"Not really 'little' anymore," Mitch offered loudly.

"Anyway..." I said, ignoring Mitch and rebooting my attempt at a flirty smile. "What do you have available?"

Andy held up a finger, grabbed a thick binder, and plopped it on the counter. "Maybe you should take a look. These are all the excursions I offer."

"Dude, how are you not sweating?" Mitch asked as I skimmed the book. "I'm from Florida and it feels like the surface of the sun here. Do Cubans not have sweat glands—"

"It says here you have a guided cable car ride with a view of the city." I pointed to a page in the book. "Are you the guide?"

"Yes I am." Andy flashed a smile.

I nodded. "Great." The perfect place to interrogate him alone, or hold him at gunpoint if he refused to talk. "We'll take that one."

CHAPTER ELEVEN

ANDY AND I STOOD next to each other inside a metal cable car with wraparound glass windows. The space was small, with no seating, so Mitch leaned against the back as we headed toward the summit of the Sierra del Rosario Mountain. The massive rocky structure rose in tumbled majesty all the way to the top.

A huge slash down the middle gave way to smaller eroded cliffs, mesas and jagged buttes, and the high elevation afforded a perfect aerial view of the southern portion of Cuba. Below, the city looked like a painting, with uncountable structures jammed together, their colors smeared and spotted, and swarms of constant traffic that weaved through city blocks like trails of ants.

Andy spoke in near-perfect English, with only the hint of a melodic accent lingering in the undertones as we rose higher. He gestured to the scenic coast. "In 1492, Christopher Columbus landed on what is now the island of Cuba and claimed it for the Kingdom of Spain. Cuba then remained a colony of Spain until the Spanish-American War of 1898, after which it came briefly under the administration of the United States until gaining formal independence in 1902..."

I was eager to shut him up. As soon as we were high enough to be out of sight, I interrupted him. "Andy. Me and my brother...we were actually hoping you could help us with something else."

Andy squinted, and his dark eyelashes seemed to thicken. "Ah...okay."

I pulled out my iPhone, flipped to a picture of Dad and extended it out. "We're looking for this man."

I watched as recognition swept across his face.

Andy shook his head, avoiding eye contact. "Sorry." His smile was unconvincing. "We get a lot of tourists—"

"We know you were his local contact," I said, getting straight to the point.

Andy's smile evaporated. "Qué relajo. What do you want?"

"He's our father." I swiped to another photo of me, Mitch and Dad. "My brother and I came here to bring him home."

"I..." Andy stammered, clearly uncomfortable.

"Listen, we're his family, we're not CIA. We have no connections to anything involved with this," I said with pleading eyes. "We just want to find our dad."

"And what is it you want from me?"

"He was here to extract someone," I answered. "Who?"

Andy paused, unable to avoid my intense gaze for long. When our eyes connected, he pressed his fingertips to his scalp and combed his hair back before turning away. He let out a deep sigh, and I could sense his reluctance, but he knew. He had a name.

"His name is Javier Castillo," he finally answered.

"We saw his picture," Mitch said. He stepped closer, biting the corner of his thumb. "Who is he?"

"Castillo is many things. Chemist, physicist, engineer."

"Why did the CIA want him extracted?" I asked.

"He is a weapons maker. His designs are revolutionary. Everyone is starting to buy from Castillo. He is the center of a very large and growing spider web—"

"What happened to my father?" I interrupted. I didn't care how good-looking this guy was. If he knew something, I'd get it out of him—by whatever means necessary.

Andy crossed his muscular biceps. "Look, you are very pretty and your brother, while a little strange..."

"Strange?" Mitch frowned.

"...seem like okay people. But I sell excursions out of a shack on the beach, comprende? What I know are bits and pieces, floating through the air that I get secondhand. I heard that he had been captured, that is it."

"How?" I asked, continuing my interrogation.

"I don't know, but honestly, does it matter how it

happened?"

"No, you're right. There's only one thing that matters—where is he now?"

Andy uncrossed his arms and turned up his palms. "Again, I'm sorry. I have no idea. Castillo has a large network in Havana. Many secret compounds and ah, what you call it...stash houses...around the city. It is impossible to know which one they have your father in. But even if you found him, it would take an army to get him out."

I nodded, thinking to myself as the cable car climbed through a cold, damp band of clouds that blotted out the tumbled slopes for a moment. Ahead, the mountain threw up its final defense, a huge slab of insurmountable jagged rock that reached the rest of the way to its apex.

"It's just the two of you?" Andy asked.

"Yes. Our father has been disavowed," I answered. "The government, the CIA...they won't even acknowledge he's here."

Andy frowned. "Then I'm sorry to say, but...you have come to Cuba for nothing, my friends."

I focused on the floor, trying to think of something we could do. I simply didn't have the resources to find him, much less break him out of any prison or compound.

"Not for nothing," I said. "I had to come. I had to try."

I stared out at the countryside as it swept beneath me. For the first time I let doubt enter my brain. I'd seen things end badly countless times in the Middle East. Valued hostages were always insulated, impossible to get to before they were taken out. With the right intel, it could be done, but I had nothing to go on. No one backing me.

The idea of never seeing my father again fully registered, and the resulting wave of emotion was so strong, it took all of my strength not to break down. Tears welled in my eyes and my throat ached with a sharp sting as I blinked them away.

I pressed my forehead to the glass, watching a second cable car approach going in the opposite direction. It was full of high school kids, laughing and having a good time. I locked eyes with a teenage girl who mimed for me to smile. But as she passed, I couldn't bring myself to do it.

The cable car full of teens headed through the fog and I remembered my own high school years. I'd taken my dad for granted then, assuming he would always be around. All that mattered to me then were my friends. But, where were they now? I hadn't spoken to any of them in years. After Mom took off, I stopped calling and so did they. They didn't understand what I was going through.

In the end, the only thing that mattered was family. Something I'd learned the hard way, and far too late. Now, Dad was gone. I'd never get to make up any of the time I'd wasted. I suddenly felt completely empty inside. As if my whole life was meaningless.

As I closed my eyes, for the briefest instant, I thought about simply going home. But I pushed the notion away. It was the only thing my childish stubborn streak was good for. *This can't be the end,* I thought and shook my head.

If Dad was alive, he'd only have a little while longer. There had to be something we could still do. As long as there was a chance, no matter how slim, I had to keep going.

And then, another thought crashed into me with equal force. Less of a thought and more of a certainty. Even if I couldn't save Dad, I would damn sure make the men who killed him pay.

"Wait a minute," Mitch said. "There still may be a way to get Dad back."

I stiffened and turned to him. "How?"

"Complete Dad's mission."

Andy squinted. "What do you mean?"

My eyes lit up as my mind chased Mitch's train of thought. Then I slapped the side of the cable car. "We don't have to find Dad or even force our way into the structures he's kept in. If we capture Castillo, we can use him as leverage to make a trade."

"Exactly," Mitch said.

"Wait, hold on—" Andy said, holding his hands up.

Mitch didn't let him finish. "Before you say anything, answer one question: Could we locate Castillo?"

Andy shrugged. "I mean, it is not uncommon to see him around the city."

"Then the impossible just became possible," I said with a smile.

"It is not uncommon, because he owns the city. All of this..." Andy motioned below. "...this is his."

I shook my head. "Doesn't matter. If we're thinking

tactically, this boils down to one single, very do-able action."

"Which is what?" Andy's skeptical eyes filled with worry.

"A kidnapping. One guy. Under the right circumstances, that's something we can do, even with our limited resources."

Andy waved his arms. "No, no, no. You do not understand. Castillo travels with armed men. You cannot just run up and grab him."

"You're right. We'd have to be smart about it." I tucked a dark lock of hair behind my ear. "This is a mission of stealth, misdirection. It can't be about force."

"Like a tiger," Mitch said.

I shot him a confused look, unable to completely hold back my smile. "Okay..."

"How does a tiger take down a buffalo, surrounded by a giant herd, all of which outweigh it by two thousand pounds?" he continued.

"I'm not playing Jeopardy with you, just tell us," I said.

"It separates the target buffalo from the rest of the pack. Then attacks it when it's vulnerable."

"The strongest opponent is weakest on the move." I nodded and turned back to Andy. I could feel my body starting to buzz with energy as I thought things through. "Do you know where Castillo lives?"

Andy shook his head. "Castillo has no home. He never sleeps in the same bed for more than a night. Very hard to track—"

I put a hand on Andy's shoulder, which shut him up. "This is our only hope. Forget everything, who this guy is, all of the obstacles. And please, just listen to what I'm saying..."

Andy's eyes softened as he looked at me. "Okay."

I realized my hand was still on his shoulder and pulled it away.

"I know it seems far-fetched, but at its core, this idea that we're proposing...is very, very simple. This is about *grabbing one guy*. I'm not saying it's easy or even realistic, but it's at least...possible."

"Yes, okay. Barely possible, like, the tiniest sliver of a possibility."

"That's enough for me. They're going to *kill* my dad. So, no matter how hard or how dangerous it is, we have to try. You understand that, right?"

"Of course. But you too must understand one thing... everyone in this city either works for Castillo or wants to. No one will help you."

"Will you?" I moved a little closer. "Help us?"

Andy's large lips parted. "Tara, listen..."

"You helped our dad. You must have had your reasons. Good reasons, right?"

Clunk. The cable car completed its journey. Mitch stepped out onto the peak of Sierra del Rosario Mountain leaving me a second more to silently plead with Andy. I waited for him to answer, but he nodded toward the open door of the cable car.

Out on the observation deck a few other groups were admiring the view. Up here it was clearer and even more breathtaking. Andy led us along the railing, stopping at the optimal point to admire the entire city of Havana sprawled out below. The metropolis of two million inhabitants was fascinating to see at this height. Full of baroque and neoclassical monuments mixed with homogeneous ensembles of private houses featuring arcades, wrought-iron gates and internal courtyards.

Andy finally turned to me. "Yes, I had my reasons. I have a special...*hatred* for the man."

"Why?" I asked.

His jaw clenched as anger flashed across his face, but he ignored my question and continued. "Aside from that, I've wanted to live in America since I was a young boy. My uncle defected, so they deny my travel visa. Harry and your government promised me safe passage and asylum in the U.S."

Mitch gripped the railing. "My father never says anything he doesn't mean," he told Andy. "Ever. Help us and he will make good on that promise."

"This is very dangerous for me. My intent was to lay low for a while. Castillo is looking for the person who helped your father in the first place. It is one of the many pieces of information they, no doubt, are trying to get from him now."

"All the more reason to help us," I urged. "Help us get him back before they figure out who you are. Then we can all get out of here."

Andy looked out at the city, thinking, then finally turned back to me. "You can stay in the safehouse I set up for your dad and I'll point you in the right direction. But that is all. Yeah?"

I nodded. "Where do we start?"

"There is a nightclub. Best in the city. Castillo is there often. It is Saturday night and the place to be, so...chances are good he will show."

Mitch shook his head. "A club? I'm too young."

Andy smiled. "No problem, my friend. Here, the legal drinking age is sixteen. Your biggest issue is getting in. Like I said, this place is very, very popular."

"Can you help us with that?" I asked.

"I know the bouncer, but..." His voice trailed off as he thought about it. "I'm trying to lay low." He scratched his cheek, clearly wanting to say something but seeming a bit uncomfortable. "Look. You are a beautiful girl. If you find something proper to wear, you won't need my help. But this place is very fancy. You'll have to dress nice."

I nodded, feeling the brushoff a little more than the compliment, but he was already giving us a place to stay so I couldn't complain too much. Maybe he wasn't a jerk or an idiot, after all.

When I glanced up, I met his eyes, and for a brief moment they were clouded with remorse.

"Come," he said, waving a hand and heading toward the cable car. "I will show you where you can stay."

After a short ride back down the mountain, Mitch and I jumped into our stolen Cadillac, and followed Andy into a neighborhood just a half-mile from the beach. Once parked, Andy led us down a beat-up road and toward a standard Cuban bodega, a breathtaking catastrophe of cheap merchandise and food.

As we headed to the front of the market, a malnourished man leaning against the wall tried to kick a skeletal dog. The mutt sidestepped the attempt and scurried off. Andy waved the man out of the way and escorted us up a wobbly set of warped stairs. The steps led to a second-story apartment directly above the bodega.

"There is one bedroom and a couch," Andy said, inviting us inside and handing me the key. "Make yourselves at home."

"Thank you," I said.

"Wait here." Andy held up a hand before disappearing into the other room. I heard the clunk of something solid against wooden floorboards. For a second, I tensed with suspicion, but then Andy came back with a metal briefcase. He set it on the dining room table. "This was your father's. I have to go back to my shack, but there are places to shop for clothes all around here. Pick out something tight and short. Be ready by 8 p.m. I will come back for you and show you the club."

"Thank you, Andy," Mitch said. "Really."

"I will get you there, and then you are on your own."

I nodded. "See you at eight."

Andy kept his eyes on me as he slipped out the door and closed it behind him. Once he was gone I walked to the briefcase and tried to open it. It was locked. There were two four-digit combinations. My eyebrows lifted slightly as an idea popped into my head. I put both Mitch and my birthdays in and tried to open it. No luck. I reversed the birthdays and *click*. The lock sprung.

Inside there were ammo clips scattered throughout. I recognized them. They belonged to a Heckler & Koch MP7A1 machine pistol and a Ruger P95 9mm. Moving them aside I pulled out a heavy waterproof plastic bag with bundles of hundred-dollar bills and a Belgian and a Nicaraguan passport, each with different names, as well as matching driver's licenses. All with Dad's picture. I shut the briefcase and let out a deep breath. It was overwhelming.

Just over my shoulder, Mitch shook his head in disbelief. "I can't even believe we're here right now."

I turned to looked around at the sparsely decorated apartment. Everything seemed old and yellowed. The only thing remotely new was an air freshener plugged into a nearby outlet that hissed out a smell meant to remind people of country breezes.

"At least we made it this far." I passed by an outdated globe on a shelf and spun it, my finger leaving a mark in the dust near Greece. "We need to be ready to go when Andy gets back," I said as Mitch plopped down on the couch, leaning back in exhaustion. "Let's come up with a plan."

CHAPTER TWELVE

A DOLLED-UP VERSION of myself stared back at me from the cracked mirror of the apartment bathroom. I'd found a girl at a local shop who got a little overly excited about giving me a Havana-style makeover. Gone were the jean shorts, tank top and sneakers. In their place, a deep maroon V-neck minidress and pair of black lace-up four-inch heels.

For an extra five bucks American, the shop girl even did my hair and make-up. My dark waves were curled and pinned, a few ringlets dangling for effect. She dusted my eyelids a smoky gray and my cheeks with a subtle blush. To cap it off, she even went to town on my nails, which now matched my dress, maroon with silver flakes along the tips.

I popped open the red lip gloss the girl threw in for free and slicked my mouth with the tiny brush from the glass tube. My lips flinched and I smacked them together. It'd been so long since I'd had a reason to dress up. It felt like a costume. Definitely a far cry from the dust-covered, sweat-soaked gear I'd sported while on tour in Iraq.

I took a step back and followed it with a deep breath, trying to decide if I liked the way I looked. Despite my demeanor, I'd never *tried* to be masculine. It sort of just took over when I joined the military. But a girl could be tough and still look good.

I leaned forward and gripped the sink with both hands, letting my head fall. It didn't matter. Getting ready was all just a distraction as I waited for the eternal minutes to pass. Every hour I wondered where he was, if it was his last, if there was still time to save him. Who knew if our plan would even work?

What sounded like a good idea a few hours earlier now seemed pretty flimsy. I'd taken part in high-value target extractions in Iraq. But every overseas mission was planned for weeks with mountains of intelligence. There were repeated run-throughs and extensive escape routes. It was all so highly coordinated. Here, we were just winging it. The whole plan felt counterintuitive to my training, the years of being taught not to do anything on impulse.

But what other choice did I have? Mitch and I were alone and Dad's life was in our hands. I swallowed down my rising fear. We were in a foreign country with no backup, no support, and no knowledge of the city itself. We also had very little knowledge of Castillo or his organization.

The more I thought it through, the more dire the situation seemed. I glanced up into the mirror. *Suck it up,* I told myself, daring my own eyes to falter. *You don't get to fall apart now.*

I let out another tense breath and touched up my eyeliner. As I stepped back and smoothed out my dress, there was a knock at the front door. I flashed my teeth to make sure they were free of lip gloss and headed to the living room.

As expected it was Andy. He stood a little too long without saying anything, his eyebrows raised.

"Wow," he finally said, clearing his throat.

Suddenly I was afraid the make-up made me look like a prostitute. "Is it too much?" I asked, embarrassment warming my already blushed cheeks.

Andy laughed. "No. It's..." His laughter faded as our eyes connected. "You look beautiful."

"Thank you," I said, breaking away from the moment.

As I stepped aside to let him in, he smelled of freshly cut pine and citrus. He wore nice jeans and leather driving shoes with a loose, white linen shirt unbuttoned at the top.

"You like nice," I said, confused by his choice in attire. "I thought you weren't coming inside with us."

He turned to sit on the sofa. "Just trying to blend in."

As he looked up, I averted my gaze. "Come on, Nancy, time to go," I shouted toward the back bedroom.

"Be right there," Mitch shouted back. "And don't call me that."

The two of us waited in silence for a moment before Andy finally spoke. "Are you sure you know what you're up against?"

"Just because I'm wearing a cocktail dress, doesn't mean I'm a bimbo. I can handle myself." I leaned in, challenging his assuming eyes, then pulled my gun out from under one of the sofa cushions. "Only one problem with a dress though..." I said. "There's nowhere to hide this."

He eyeballed the gun, and I wished I could hear what he was thinking.

"For the record," he said. "I know you're not a *bimbo.* Not many men, let alone young women, would come here to do what you're doing. But there is a line, as they say, between brave and reckless."

His concerned expression made me turn my focus to the floor.

"And you'll have to keep your weapon in the car," he added. "They are very strict at the club. They will frisk you and search your purse. That's why I got you this..."

I glanced up, surprised as Andy stood and pulled a silver necklace from his pocket. He dangled it from his palm and I stepped forward to get a better look. At the end was a beautifully ornate dragon, its tail curving another few inches down. Once we were feet apart he grabbed the tail and yanked it, pulling the pendant in half to reveal a small, hidden knife.

I set my gun on the coffee table and smiled. "Wow," I said, reaching out to examine it. The details were intricate and there was a nice weight to it. "It's beautiful."

"And sharp. I didn't feel right about you going in unprotected." He reached a hand out. "Here. I'll help you put it on."

I handed him the necklace and turned my back to him, feeling slightly guilty for thinking he was a jerk. "Thank you," I said quietly.

As he draped the chain around my neck, I became acutely aware of how close we were, a few inches apart at most. His hand brushed my bare shoulder and instant goosebumps rose on my arms, the space between us growing warm and strangely intimate.

"You know, I can get it," I said, reaching back.

"Just stay still." The chain brushed my collarbone and as the tips of his fingers tickled the back of my neck, I tensed up. He locked the clasp. "There, all set."

I turned back around, letting out a slow shaky breath as Andy adjusted the dragon.

"Listen," I said, desperately searching for a segue. "I just wanted to thank you for your help. I, we...my brother and I...appreciate it."

"You are welcome."

We stood facing each other, until I turned to look down the hallway for Mitch. He was taking his sweet time. "Hurry up, Mitch!" I yelled.

I turned back to Andy, intentionally moving out of his personal space. "So, did you know my father well?"

"No, no. I spent a little time with him, but not much.

He seemed like a good man. Very honest, straight-forward."

"He is the best man I know."

"I respect what you are trying to do. I know if it was my father, I would move mountains to save him."

I glanced at the gun on the table. "I'll do whatever I have to."

"Do you have a plan?" he asked.

Mitch and I had discussed it earlier. It wasn't full-proof, but it was the best we could do. "We follow him home. See where he's staying. If he's switching homes every couple days, maybe we get lucky and he's at one we can sneak into. Maybe, just maybe there's a security breach, an opening, or a patrol change. Something. Something that would let us grab him as he sleeps..."

Mitch stepped in from the hallway, his hair still wet. "You guys aren't much for water pressure around here are you?" He tugged at a dark blue silk shirt that hung over black pants.

"You look good my friend," Andy said. "But we need to go."

ANDY DROPPED US off in our stolen Cadillac some distance from the club and pointed us toward the line.

"Popular place," I said as I slid out of the car in my slinky dress.

"Sorry I can't come with you. I'm just trying to—"

"Lay low," I finished for him. "Yeah, I know."

"You shouldn't have any problem getting in, though," he said through the open window. "You look amazing."

"Thanks." I waved a hand at him, then Mitch and I made our way across the street to the humming crowd of waiting people.

The façade of the Vida Futura Nightclub was a stunning spectacle. Completely encircling the top railing of the modern two-story building, torches plumed with five-foot-high flames. Behind them, women in elaborate costumes and headdresses danced erotically to an intense chill-pop and flamenco mash-up beat. The women had curves upon curves and I quietly laughed to myself at how their swaying hips seemed to hypnotize Mitch.

The dancers were entertaining for the first hour. After that their taunting movements made me increasingly irritated. When we finally reached the front, the enormous bouncer peered at me from under dark, bushy eyebrows.

"Él está contigo?" he growled, nodding at Mitch.

I bit my lip, not understanding.

"Is he with you?" he repeated, crossing his tattooed forearms over his chest.

I smiled sweetly. "Him? Oh, yeah. He's with me."

The bouncer looked away and waved his hand for us to exit the line. "Sorry. Not tonight."

"Wait," I pleaded. "We need to get in there."

He glared at me as I continued to plead and finally waved some of his guys over to escort us away.

"Come on. I have money," I whispered. "Isn't there—"

"Carlos!" Andy's voice carried over the crowd as he jogged forward. "*Acere, qué bolá?*"

The bouncer extended a fist, which he bumped.

Without warning Andy put an arm around my back, resting his hand on my hip. I tensed and stared at it for a moment, suddenly feeling my heartbeat everywhere. But the bouncer waved his guys off and I smiled.

"Sorry I'm late, Baby." He gave me quick wide-eyed look, silently telling me to play along.

"That's okay."

I leaned into him, secretly enjoying the contact and the smell of his cologne, then wrapped my arm around his firm torso. My hand stopped at his waist, and I could feel the side of his abdominal muscles contracting as he stepped forward.

"Is this tu novia?" Carlos asked, his serious features now light with friendly familiarity.

"Sí. Can we get in tonight?"

Andy smiled and led me up to a velvet rope, sliding his arm down to grab hold of my hand.

"Just her?"

"And her brother," Andy said.

"Another guy?" The bouncer looked down the waiting line. "It is tough tonight."

"It is tough every night, come on Carlos," he nodded toward me. "Don't let me down. It is her brother's birthday, she wants to make sure he has fun."

"All right, but then we're even."

The bouncer removed the rope. Andy patted him on the back and motioned to Mitch who ran up.

"You two are in, just make sure you tip my friend on the way out, yes?"

"We will, thanks," I said as we headed inside.

As Mitch made his way into the club, I stopped Andy in the entry.

"You didn't have to do that," I said, "but thank you. Were you watching from somewhere?"

He shook his head. "No, I came back. I couldn't let you do this by yourself."

"What about laying low?"

I turned to check on Mitch who was waiting in the dimly lit hallway up ahead.

"I'll keep my head down," Andy answered.

I sighed, reluctant to accept more help. "Andy—"

"Follow me," he said, keeping hold of my hand.

"What's going on?" Mitch asked as we passed.

I ignored the question, knowing Mitch would trail behind as we headed into the club. After navigating a series of corridors, we exited into the main space. It was enormous inside and packed with people all swaying in rhythm. The decor mixed the old with the new. Classic Cuban paintings, fixtures and columns blended seamlessly among strange, modern furniture tortured into strange shapes, all feathered together with bold, colored lighting throughout.

After the patdown Andy warned me about, I realized I'd lost sight of Mitch. I walked in, paused and took in the rest of the space. It was insane, unlike anything I'd ever experienced. I had been in a few clubs, but they were nothing like this.

The main dance floor was entirely see-through with what looked like molten lava coursing back and forth underneath. Colored lights played over it, turning it into a multicolored ocean of acid blues, stark greens, and hot pinks. Girls tossed long hair and boys pumped fists. Slender limbs appeared and disappeared as the masses danced. Above, the entire second floor was ringed with a giant metal railing. A massive throng pressed against it, like a riot crowd held back by a security fence. They all pulsed to the music. Even those engaging in casual conversations reflexively moved to the beat.

"We lost Mitch," I shouted to Andy.

He stopped and a pack of stunning, but clearly intoxicated women stumbled toward us, their bodies shimmering with gold necklaces and chunky neon rings. The girls giggled loudly, their insanely short skirts riding dangerously high. They swarmed around us like bees passing a tree, coagulating on the other side and bouncing out onto the dance floor.

Andy leaned in close to my ear. "Do you see him?"

I took a deep breath as I searched, and a swirl of smells assaulted me. Perfume mixed with the spice of dribbled bourbon and the tang of mixed drinks, all being pumped around the room by high-powered air conditioners designed to keep the frenetic mob inside from sweating. I finally spotted Mitch through the crowd. He was leaning up against the bar, holding a beer.

I tugged on Andy's hand and walked up to him. "Really?"

"Hey, we've got to blend in."

Mitch glanced at the two of us holding hands and I immediately let go.

"Come on," Andy said to both of us. "Let's get a better vantage point."

We followed him along a set of glowing, sweeping, rounded stairs, up to the second floor. I found a spot near the railing and pressed against it, my eyes skimming the area. Andy stepped up next to me and Mitch took the spot to my right before downing a big swig of beer.

I pushed his bottle down. "One beer. And nurse it. We're not here for fun."

"Dad lets me have one every night. Helps me relax."

"First off, I don't believe you and second, you're a sheltered suburban teenager, what could you possibly be stressed about?"

"My psychologist says I get raised levels of generalized anxiety in situations where I have no obvious control."

I laughed. "Fine, Nancy. Have a beer if you really need it."

The three of us stared straight ahead in silence as I scanned the club, checking every face.

Another few seconds went by before Mitch spoke again. "You know what kills me?" he said, the beer clearly starting to loosen his tongue. "All this time I was trying to be the good son, trying to be like Dad. But the whole time, he was more like you."

I laughed at the irony. "And I thought I didn't fit in with you two squares."

Andy stepped away from the railing and I turned. "With the size of this place, we should split up," he said.

"Good idea," I answered. "Let's start downstairs. Mitch, you stay here." I glanced at the near-empty beer bottle. "Like, don't move from this exact spot."

He rolled his eyes. "Yeah, I got it," he said, holding his beer up in a mock toast.

As I serpentined my way through the crowd and downstairs, Andy followed me, despite our original plan to split up. After a few minutes of wading through heated bodies, dodging loosely held drinks and sharp heels, he pointed to a small table on the far end of the club.

"I'm going to sit there, out of view," he said.

"Okay," I shouted, but before I turned to head in another direction, I jerked at the sight of Castillo in my peripheral vision. I rushed closer to get a better look as he walked by with an entourage. It was definitely him. The man looked almost frail next to his eight large bodyguards. I watched as word of Castillo's arrival spread, buzzing down rows of club-goers like a line of firecrackers.

After a few minutes, Mitch found us and sat down at

the table.

"We saw him," I said immediately. "Just keep calm. Let me think this through."

Castillo was led toward a roped-off VIP area full of plush velvet couches less than fifty feet away. At this distance, he looked older than his picture, which must have been taken years ago. He was probably sixty-five if I had to guess. His skin was pockmarked, scarred and much rougher in this light. The overhead glow cast a shadow into each dimple. His white hair was slicked nicely to the side, which did nothing to hide his age. He walked with a distinct gait and carried himself with an air of entitlement. I glared at him, unbridled rage burning in my chest. The man who held my father's life in his hands sat fifty feet away.

Castillo headed into the VIP area, tugged at the sleeves of his shirt and sat down on one of the couches.

"So now we just wait for him to leave, right?" Mitch asked. He had nothing to fidget with so he wrung his hands and popped his knuckles. "Just follow him home..."

Mitch trailed off as five teenage girls were roughly escorted up to the VIP section and lined up in front of Castillo.

When he turned, I noticed his right arm was normal, but his left one was shriveled and missing the thumb. A birth defect had, in essence, turned his hand into a claw. It was what he used to take liberties with the women, who almost seemed in a fugue state. As he ran his claw along their bodies, his smile glittered like poisonous water.

I resisted the urge to stand and go after him. "Yes, we wait," I answered, clenching my teeth and biting back my impatience.

For the next several hours I sat, watching, filled with disgust, but ready to move. The club became a distant rumble of sound, and my eyes stayed focused on the target. They took in each shameful grope, each hungry glance, his well-fed, satisfied smirk.

When he finally tired of the women, he got to his feet, shaking one of them off like a clingy child.

"He's leaving," I said, moving for the exit before the guys had time to respond.

"Okay, just don't—" Andy started, but I was already winding through the crowd.

CHAPTER THIRTEEN

I PULLED THE OLD-SCHOOL Cadillac "Yank Tank" down a side road and positioned it toward the club. Castillo's vehicles weren't hard to spot. Three identical Cadillac Escalades waited for him out front. He took his time exiting, and I gripped the steering wheel, my anger refreshed as he ambled toward the cars, his armed men in tow.

Andy sat in the back seat. I could feel his hesitant eyes through the rearview, but he kept quiet.

Mitch cracked his knuckles next to me. "Dude has a convoy." He shook his head too many times and I could sense his anxiety spiking. "I don't know, man."

"The vehicles are armored too," I said, squinting.

"How do you know?" Andy asked.

I pointed. "They're easy to spot. See, the metal's thicker

at the seams."

The three SUVs pulled out onto the street in a perfect line, their headlights quickly sweeping past and flaring to white. The light shined across Mitch's face, creating shadows beneath his cheekbones. I waited a few heart-pounding seconds, then slipped in behind them, maintaining a safe distance. Far enough to keep them in sight, but not close enough to arouse suspicion.

Less than a mile from the club, the SUVs began to systematically change positions, front to back, side to side.

"What the heck are they doing?" Mitch asked.

"I told you," Andy said, leaning forward through the two front seats. "It is not possible to catch this man."

"Relax," I shifted in my seat, refusing to be outwitted. "All convoys do that in case they're being watched. That way you don't know which one the target's in."

Mitch tapped his fidgety fingers on the armrest. "Like a giant shell game."

"Right," I said, my eyes locking on the second to the last car. "Except I was always good at that."

After another couple miles, we came to a four-way stop. Instead of turning in unison, all three SUVs headed in opposite directions.

Mitch turned to me, chewing into the pad of his thumb. "Either this is standard protocol or they know someone's following them. Right?"

I kept my gaze forward. "Doesn't matter. This only helps us. They've separated, and I know which one

Castillo's in."

Andy placed his hand on my shoulder, and I tensed like a muzzled dog. "If they know they are being followed, you need to turn back," he said.

I risked a quick glance in the rearview mirror and our eyes connected for a moment. He was right, but we didn't know for sure they were on to us. We still had a shot.

"We have what we wanted," I said, turning left and following one of the SUVs. "He's isolated down to one car."

"The one you *think* he's in." Andy removed his hand, but his accented words swept over my shoulder like a tangible cloud of reason.

My eyes narrowed as I focused on the Escalade ahead of us. "This might be our only chance."

Logic was a pesky gnat I chose to swat away. The only person on the planet capable of stopping my father's death was in that car. If we'd been spotted, I had to act now while the Escalade was alone. We couldn't wait for him to reach his destination and his armed team of backup. I locked my jaw and stomped the accelerator.

"Castillo's in this one, I know it," I said as the car lurched forward and gained speed. The Yank tank ate asphalt as the automatic transmission ground through new gears.

Mitch turned, confused. "What are you doing?"

"Put on your seat belt."

"Listen to me," he yelled. "Be smart about this."

"Sit back and shut up."

I kept the accelerator down and quickly caught up to the Escalade, getting within a hundred yards of the bumper. Then eighty, then seventy, sixty, fifty.

"Stop the car!" Mitch shouted.

The Escalade was coming up fast. Forty, thirty, twenty. If I could just get them off the road...

Mitch reached over and grabbed the steering wheel, turning it to avoid the crash. The car swerved and slid into on-coming traffic. For the briefest second, I froze, waiting for the crunch and shatter of impact, but before my next breath, instinct took over.

I yanked the wheel and the car did a 180. It slid sideways, barely avoiding the first on-coming car. I steered into the farthest lane, the tires reaching the limits of adhesion before I deftly jerked onto the far shoulder of the road. Reapplying the brakes, I regained control before finally skidding to a halt. The front end of the car stopped within inches of a telephone pole and then rocked slowly backward.

I pounded the wheel and spun toward Mitch. "What the hell were you doing?" I yelled.

"The right thing," Mitch, shouted back. "What were you going to do, ram their car?"

"For starters!"

"You might be a good driver, but think through the physics. That SUV has an extra ton, plus an anti-rolled suspension. If by some miracle, you got them to stop, they're armored and the glass is bullet proof. Even if Castillo is in there, we'd never get him out!"

"He was alone," I argued. "This was an opportunity. Who knows where he's going or how many guys will be there?"

"Tell yourself whatever you want. But the element of surprise was the only advantage we had and you probably just blew it."

I turned away, shifting uncomfortably in my tiny dress. He was right, which only made me angrier. I'd been reckless, disregarding my training and everything I knew in the heat of the moment. It was a bad call.

"Whatta you want me to say?" I muttered, still defensive.

"I don't want you to *say* anything. I want—"

"Um, guys..." Andy interrupted.

I took a breath and bit back my anger, hoping to end the conversation. "What?" I snapped.

I glanced at him, his large green eyes wide with alarm. One of Castillo's black Escalades had circled around. Andy turned to watch out the rear windshield as the SUV sped toward us. My adrenaline spiked. I might have been right about which car Castillo was in, but just like Mitch said, we had now identified ourselves as a threat.

The Escalade picked up speed, clearly intent on plowing right through us. Out of sheer panic, I gunned the car. It peeled out, kicking up rocks along the gravel shoulder, but got us out of the way of the Escalade, which missed us just barely and slammed the telephone pole with such force, the hood folded into a V-shape and put the vehicle out of commission.

I pulled forward, speeding back onto the road, and cranked the wheel hard to get the old car pointed in the right direction. As I straightened out, a second Escalade appeared from behind. I floored the car, but wouldn't be able to outrun it. I glanced ahead to scout an alternate route, when another Escalade appeared from the opposite direction. They had all circled back.

A dark-skinned man with an automatic weapon leaned out of the oncoming Escalade and my pulse quickened. He was about to fire. I twisted the wheel hard then jerked the parking break, a maneuver Vince and I used to do for fun in empty parking lots after a few drinks. The creaking Yank tank spun into a ninety-degree, hard right turn. The tactic was awkward in this old car, but it worked as I released the brake, floored the accelerator and rocketed down a side road.

"We're in trouble, we're in so much trouble," Mitch said, his eyes as wide as saucers.

I glanced back at Andy who was pinned to the back seat.

"Relax," I said loudly, though my hands were slick against the wheel. "Getting away in stolen cars was pretty much my job in high school."

The two Escalades slid in behind me, giving chase. The first one caught up and rammed us from behind, which threw the car into an uncontrolled spin. Scenery smeared past the window and I could hardly breathe, but somehow my body still knew what to do, like muscle memory. I let my foot off the accelerator, and used perfect rhythm between the brake and steering wheel to pull out of the spin. It always amazed me how capable I could become when my survival was at stake.

As we slid to a stop, the sudden deceleration caused me to lurch forward against my straining seat belt shoulder strap. The taut fabric cut into my flesh like a band of steel.

I spun the wheel and put all my weight back onto the accelerator, sliding onto a large, main street. Only instead of finding open road, I was immediately slowed by a milling crowd.

"Shit, where are we?" I asked as waves of tourists jumped out of the way of our car. "It's some sort of art festival or something."

"Paseo del Prado," Andy blurted, "the first paved street of Havana."

"Thank you, Mr. Tour Guide," I said, "but which way do I go? Where's the nearest street?"

"Take the next right."

I nosed the car onto the paved marble walkway that divided the lanes, determined to escape, whatever it took.

Andy winced at me through the rearview. "Ay, I meant at the light, Tara."

The steering wheel vibrated and the dashboard rattled as I took on the shallow curb meant for pedestrian entry. "You said the next right!"

I managed my way back onto the roadway and veered down a perpendicular street. Dodging pedestrians had slowed us down, and the two Escalades hadn't been afraid to follow. They were right on our bumper.

"Come on, come on," I muttered, my eager foot pressing slightly harder on the pedal.

I sped up as the crowd lightened and blew through a red light. In my mirrors, I watched cars from either direction lock brakes, screeching across asphalt. The closest trailing Escalade split the two cars, but clipped the front ends of both, sending them spiraling away.

"Holy..." Mitch shouted, as I let out a deep breath.

The second Escalade passed through the shower of metal and glass as I turned down an alley. I tore through to the next street and slid sideways onto it, working the brake pedal the way an angler worked a fishing reel. With the accelerator pinned I flew down the road with the Escalades close behind. The two cars bobbed and weaved, took simultaneous lefts and rights. I couldn't shake them. I veered around slower vehicles and blared my horn as I shot through another red light and multiple lanes of traffic.

Ahead, an oblivious driver stopped so suddenly I had to whip the wheel and turn again into oncoming traffic. This time, I couldn't pull out. Instead, I weaved through a swarming constellation of cars, every one a potential deadly weapon. I finally caught an opening and whipped back into the correct lane.

After a few more minutes, I finally made it into a more residential neighborhood. With the Escalades looming in my rearview, I made a hard right down a small side road. The thick trees on all sides sucked them in, tunnel-like. Immediately, I saw the giant, thick metal gate up ahead. Behind it were giant mansions. It was a dead-end.

I squinted in forced concentration. This was a private, gated community for the very rich. Which meant, that gate was not going to give. It had to be reinforced. There was no way to ram through it, especially not with the ancient car I was driving. It would fold like an accordion.

I slammed on the brakes and skidded to a stop. Tire smoke billowed. Behind us, the two Escalades spread out to block the entire road, most likely knowing the gate was immovable. My gut felt heavy with defeat.

"What are you doing?" Mitch asked.

"That gate's reinforced, no way we get through it," I said.

Mitch spun in his seat staring at the Escalades bearing down on us. The SUVs took up the entire width of the tree-lined road. He glanced back at the gate, his eyes ticking back and forth as if his mind had slipped into overdrive.

My heart drummed against my rib cage and beads of

sweat formed on my brow. "I have to turn around, go right at them. Play chicken. Hope one of the drivers blinks."

Andy lurched forward. "Estas loca?"

"Wait!" Mitch said, his eyes focused in front of us.

"Wait for what? We're out of options." Loose curls from my done-up hair had fallen into my face, and I swept them away, crazed with desperation.

"Go for the gatehouse."

Andy looked back and forth between the two of us. "What?"

"It's wood," Mitch answered. "There's no permanent foundation. It's a structural weakness."

I pressed my lips together in thought, anxiety coursing through me like engine oil. "I wanna disagree with you, but the truth is...I don't have a better idea."

I forced the accelerator to the floor and the car picked up speed. Twenty yards from the gate, I saw someone inside the gatehouse. I laid on the horn, and a man looked up as I twisted the wheel and made right for him.

"Move!" I screamed, though I was sure he couldn't hear me.

He scrambled to his feet and dove out the side door moments before I smashed through. I winced as the gatehouse exploded around us, but just as Mitch predicted, the Yank tank punched a hole between the metal gate and the cement wall. A torrent of debris fanned across the windshield as the car slammed down onto the other side.

I looked behind me to see the Escalades skid to a stop. They couldn't make it through the gate and their vehicles were too wide to pass through the hole we'd just made. They simply couldn't follow.

As I drove the car away, Mitch kept watch behind us.

He spun back around in his seat and breathed a giant sigh of relief. "We're in the clear."

My chest finally relaxed, though tension still racked my body.

After a few silent moments, Andy leaned slowly forward, staring at me in shock. "You are completely insane."

I glanced over my shoulder, regretting getting him involved. I could have gotten him killed. "Look, I'm sorry—" I started to apologize.

"I don't know where you learned to drive like that," Andy said with a playful grin. "But I think I'm in love with you."

CHAPTER FOURTEEN

DESPITE MITCH'S INITIAL PANIC that we were trapped inside the gated community, lady luck finally blessed us with the tiniest gift—an exit. After winding our way through the wealthy suburb, dense with palms and Spanish colonial homes, we found a second gatehouse. As it did for all residents, the automatic wrought-iron fence sensed our vehicle and rolled to the side as we approached, allowing our vehicle to pass.

Mitch threw his back into the seat, sighing a deep breath of relief and Andy navigated us to the apartment in near silence.

"Park far away and out of sight," he said as we got closer. "Just in case someone spots the car."

I nodded and parked on the gravel near the dumpster-side of another rundown apartment building two streets down.

"So, what now?" Mitch asked, vocalizing the question I'd been quietly mulling over in my head.

I didn't have an answer.

When I held my silence, he shook his head and shot out of the car, slamming the door behind him.

Andy stayed quiet as I stared past the steering wheel, obsessing over my mistake.

Finally, I caught his sorrowful eyes in the rearview mirror. "Do you think the club—"

He shook his head. "He won't be at the club again. Not after what just happened."

I nodded, trying to shove the gut-wrenching disappointment somewhere deep.

"Hey." Andy reached out, placing his warm hand on my bare shoulder. "Maybe I can talk with some people. Like I said, everyone either knows him or works for him in this city."

I turned in my seat, torn at the thought of putting him in more danger, but also desperate. "You're supposed to be laying low. I can't keep asking—"

"You're not asking." He leaned in closer. "I'm offering. And I can be subtle. There are ways to get answers to questions without asking directly. I'll worry about me. You worry about your Dad...and Mitch."

"Thank you," I said, resisting the urge to hug him. It was a long-shot, but at least it was something.

Andy smiled, staring at me so long I almost thought he might kiss me, but Mitch pounded on the window.

"Come on," he yelled through the glass. "Let's go."

"Get some rest." Andy opened his door. "I'll come by the safehouse if I get any information that might help."

THAT NIGHT, THE only thing to do was wait and hope. After I explained Andy's plan, Mitch barely spoke a word to me and eventually passed out on the couch, leaving me to stare at the bedroom ceiling.

Without realizing I'd fallen asleep, I jolted awake hours later, gasping and lurching toward someone who wasn't there. Blinking my eyes to clear the tears, I sat upright in bed, reliving the nightmare. My pulse slowed as I let out a heavy breath, but I couldn't wipe the image of my dead father from my mind. What if I'd ruined our only chance? What if they killed him because of me?

I swallowed down the sting in my throat, ignoring the sharp whispers of doubt that taunted me. Either way I wouldn't quit, not until I got answers. Proof of his death, revenge, *something*.

I couldn't rely wholly on Andy. Mitch and I needed a backup plan.

Slowly rolling my legs off the bed, I craned my neck forward until I heard the satisfying crack of vertebrae. My body felt stiff from last night's action. Hoping a shower would help, I headed to the bathroom, letting the dribbling water run for a minute before finally hopping in.

It was possible Castillo and his men hadn't got a good

look at us. Maybe we still had some portion of the element of surprise. If Andy's offer was serious, and we could narrow down Castillo's location, maybe we could try grabbing him again. Be smarter about it. Or, maybe I'd allowed my emotion to get the best of me, spooked them all and set off an unthinkable conclusion.

I ducked my head under the weak stream and allowed the lukewarm water to run down my body. It was a poor excuse for a shower, but at least the tepid water woke me up and helped me think.

I turned and wet my midsection, my lower back throbbing with tension. I hadn't realized my muscles were so tight. Grabbing a washcloth, I went to work on the thick layer of mascara still caked to my eyelashes.

Once my face was makeup-free, I stared down at my chest. A diagonal bruise ran from my left shoulder to my right hip, compliments of the seat belt. I stared at it for a second, marveling at the different shades of bright green, deep blue and brown. It made me think of Dad, and I couldn't help wonder what sort of torture he'd endured.

I rinsed and dried off quickly, slipping into the new jean shorts and T-shirt I'd bought when I purchased the dress. Taking a deep breath, I prepared myself mentally to face Mitch. I shuffled down the hallway, my feet padding across the cheap, worn apartment carpet, ready to apologize again. Only, as I stepped into the living room, Mitch was gone. The knot in my stomach tightened. *Where was he?*

As I turned to the kitchen, I saw a note on the counter:

Went for a run. Need to get my head around what happened last night. Don't do anything until I get back. We'll discuss a game plan.

Immediately I pulled out my phone to call him, but it rang ten feet away from me in the corner of the couch where he'd slept.

I crumpled up the note and sat on one of the bar stools, annoyed he felt so overly confident here. What if they'd seen our faces? They were probably looking for us. He couldn't just take off on a run in the middle of all this without his phone. He didn't even have the basic training needed to defend himself if attacked.

My dream resurfaced, and the image of Dad in some tiny cell, beaten and bloodied ran through my head. Then my mind put Mitch in the same horrifying scenes. I pressed my lips together as guilt dug its claws deep into my chest. My eyes threatened tears, but I cut them off quickly.

I shook my arms. *Focus.* I needed to make some progress, fast. Step one was finding Mitch. I had no idea how long he'd been gone. Maybe he'd run to Andy's hut. It was the only familiar thing in the area.

I uncrumpled his note and used the pen on the counter to write a message back to him.

"Went looking for you. Call me if you get back before

me."

I put his cell phone next to it and grabbed mine, shoving it in the back pocket of my jean shorts along with a small wad of cash.

Hoping Mitch would be back soon, I left the door unlocked and closed it behind me. Outside, the air hung thick with tempting morning smells floating out of the short string of cafés around the corner. I eyed the plates of patrons salivating over their torrejas, the Cuban version of French toast, a pork and plantain breakfast hash followed by stuffed arepas and of course Cuban espresso.

I couldn't help myself. Mitch and I had been eating junk from the convenience store below our safehouse. I stopped at one of the restaurants, doing my best to point and order a breakfast that Mitch and I could share when I found him. Then, remembering Andy, I ordered him some random thing off the menu and a coffee. He was the one source of possible intel I had at this point, and I was praying he had something else for me to go on.

As I made for the beach, my thoughts chased themselves like birds trapped in an attic. I stopped at the curb and checked my phone, struggling to hold the food with one hand.

Nothing.

I sighed and kept walking.

When the ocean came into view I caught sight of a family of four slogging through the sand to find a spot. The two children, a brother and sister, carried buckets and shovels, and their parents held armfuls of towels and folding chairs. Everywhere I looked I was reminded of Dad.

I had spent so much time trying to be independent, and now I'd give anything for one more day, one more moment with him. He'd been my anchor, from the minute I was born. Before things fell apart for us as a family, Mom used to tell me a story. I could still hear the sound of her voice, alto-deep, like a hummed lullaby.

"He would try to talk to you before you were even born," she would say. "He would open my mouth and say, 'Hello, how's it going down there?'" We'd laugh at her impression of Dad. "And he'd tell you stories, too. Late at night, he'd lay his head against my belly and talk to you."

Apparently, I'd heard him inside Mom's stomach, because minutes after I was born, Dad asked the doctor if I was okay. And, as the story went, my eyes started scanning the room, looking for him, like I already knew him.

Now here I was in some strange land, searching for him again.

I trudged through the thick, hot sand with my armful of food. Thankfully, Andy was there, sitting in the depths of his excursion shack. But Mitch was nowhere in sight. I shuffled over and set the bagged breakfast and coffee onto the shelf next to his head. He looked up from a book and his face brightened.

"Hola," he said, standing.

"Hola." I glanced around, slightly unnerved at the

idea of Castillo's men out looking for us. "Are you sure you should be out here?" I asked, slipping into a shadowed corner of his hut. "Chances are one of his guys got a look at our faces."

"Yes, but if not, disappearing looks more suspicious. I have...obligations. I can't just abandon my life."

"I get that." I nodded, trying to keep hidden. "So, about the whole 'me almost getting you killed thing...'" I slid over his breakfast and flashed him a please-forgive-me smile. "I'm really sorry. I brought you something called pabellon criollo and coffee."

"Sí." His eyes widened in mock amusement. "Almost dying was...fun." Although his voice was heavy with sarcasm, he grabbed the coffee and took a sip. "Gracias." The coffee wet his upper lip and he wiped it with his thumb. "Maybe we should do it again sometime. Do you have plans tonight?"

I laughed, taking his lightheartedness as an accepted apology. "That depends. I may be out searching for my lost little brother." I scanned the beach but didn't see him. "Did Mitch come by here? He left a note saying he went for a run."

"No." Andy's brow furrowed with concern. "But he's fine. I am sure—"

My ringing phone interrupted him.

I reached for it with anxious fingers and let out a sigh of relief. "It's him," I said before answering. "Mitch, you can't just take off like that. They could have seen your face.

It's not safe—"

He cut me off, giving me some spiel about a panic attack and letting off steam.

"Well…just stay there," I snapped, unable to keep my frustration from slipping out. "I'm coming back." I tapped the end call button and rolled my eyes. "He's at the apartment."

"Good," Andy said, but his focus was on something else. He took my hand, and turned it palm up. There was a bruise on my forearm from all the banging around in the car last night. Andy brushed it lightly with his thumb, sending chills up to my shoulder. I swallowed and pulled my hand away.

"It's nothing." My mind scrambled for traction, distracted by his touch. "Listen," I said, trying to regain my focus. "If my father has any chance, I've got to find him soon. Did you hear anything?"

Andy shook his head. "I've reached out to a few trusted friends, but nothing."

The ocean seemed to grow louder in the distance, its crashing waves beating the shore with steady persistence as I processed the disappointment.

Before I could respond, Andy turned at the sight of Jorge, the man with the Mohawk who had been shaking him down the day before.

"Who is this guy?" I asked.

Andy's eyes turned serious. "You should go—"

"Do you have it?" Jorge asked, leaning against the

front of the shack.

Andy took a step back. "Jorge. Por favor. Maybe we could do this another time, yes?"

"You don't tell me when we do this. When I come, that's when we do this. Now where's my money?"

"I told you, this stand doesn't make enough. I am barely getting by—"

"Bullshit," Jorge yelled, then calmed himself.

He grabbed Andy's coffee and took a big sip. As he lowered it, he paused catching sight of me in the shadowed corner of the shack. He cocked his head sideways and sucked his teeth. "Who's this fine young thing?"

"Just a customer."

Jorge smiled at me exposing a dead tooth. His left front incisor was completely, repulsively—gray.

I stared back at him, apparently making it a little too obvious that he made me want to vomit.

"I don't like the way she's looking at me," Jorge hissed.

"And I don't like...your tooth," I responded without thinking.

He frowned and tossed the coffee to the ground. "What'd you say, Bitch?"

I stepped outside the shack. With men like Jorge, it was important not to show weakness.

"My Dad told me once that you can take the measure of a man by the way he treats people. Which makes you a real piece of garbage."

I was hoping to embarrass him enough that he'd walk

away, but Jorge went for a backhanded slap instead. Reacting out of instinct, I grabbed his wrist and bent his arm backward, the ligaments in his elbow popping with a sickening crack. Before he could scream, I drove the back of my hand into his throat and sent him down into the sand.

The minute he fell, I stepped back, upset with myself for losing control. I winced, as Andy stood there, completely stunned.

"I'm sorry—"

"You..." Jorge said, still gasping.

I bent down, helping him to a sitting position. "Lean forward. It'll help get your wind back."

As Jorge sat up completely, he pulled a gun out of an ankle holster. I cursed myself for not checking and took another step back.

"You messed up big time," he said, slowly getting to his feet. He fumbled for something tucked into his back pocket and thrust a badge in front of me.

Perfect, I thought. Of course he was a cop.

CHAPTER FIFTEEN

I THOUGHT ABOUT RUNNING, of punching Jorge right in his dead, ugly-toothed mouth and taking off, and I probably would have if not for the gun. The pompous sneer he wore when shoving me into his rinky-dink police car with its lone, pathetic blue light on top, made me want to head butt him in the nose, but I couldn't help my Dad if I was dead. I'd have to talk my way out of this, which mostly meant keeping my mouth shut, something I found extremely hard to do when it came to a-holes like Jorge.

After we reached the local precinct, a dirty brick building with the words *Policía Nacional Revolucionaria* above the door, my prints were taken, and I was escorted to a small interrogation room. Jorge handcuffed me to a metal I-ring bolted to the top of a stainless-steel table and left me there. The room had a low acoustic-tile ceiling, drab green walls, and a single window, which was clearly a two-way mirror.

I stared at myself in the reflection as I waited, not knowing if anyone was on the other side. Not caring. I'd lost. Too much time had passed and there was nothing I could do about any of it now. Defeat coaxed me to the edge. *Give up*, it whispered. I could already feel the numbness spreading, deadening all the branches of budding hope in my heart.

It was over. Dad was gone. Whatever happened to me didn't matter.

As I looked into my own deadpan eyes, one thing sparked the last shred of emotion in me. If Dad was really gone, Castillo had gotten away with it. He'd killed one of the two people I loved most in the world, and kept living his scumbag life, taking advantage of girls and acting like the king of Cuba. I ground my teeth, subtly testing the strength of the chain securing my cuffed wrists.

After nearly an hour of waiting I began to feel like a trapped animal, the urge to thrash and scream nearly boiling to the surface. I thought about Mitch. What would he do if anything happened to me? How would he get home? Would Castillo find him?

The panic crept up the back of my neck until my shoulders locked and tensed. My breath quickened. I had to get out of here.

Just as I was about to call out, the door opened and in walked a distinguished-looking man with thick black hair, salted with white along the sides, and overgrown wiry eyebrows. His small nose and weak chin made his teeth seem more prominent. They were barely covered by full lips ringed by a well-manicured goatee.

Jorge walked behind him, his arm in a sling.

"You messed up my arm, Yuma," Jorge barked, jabbing his finger over the man's shoulder.

The officer turned to him in annoyance. "Jorge, wait outside."

"What? Why?"

The man stared at Jorge until he reluctantly backed out of the room and shut the door.

"Name's Nefasto," he said, sitting opposite me.

I didn't respond, but watched as he ripped a rectangle into a pack of cigarettes and shook one out. He tapped the tip on the tabletop and blew on the end of the filter before pumping it into his mouth then caught me staring at him.

"A superstition from my youth. A friend once told me if you blow on the filter, it will get rid of any stray microscopic synthetic fibers. Apparently, that's what does the most damage to your lungs."

"Oh, really," I said, testing out a shy smile. Playing innocent was my best bet. If I could pull off the apologetic tourist, maybe he'd let me go.

Nefasto extended the pack toward me. "Cigarette, Ms. Kafee?"

My eyes lifted, and I couldn't hide the surprise in them. "How'd you know my name?"

"You're American. I have connections and ran your

prints. Wasn't hard." He smiled, and tossed his pack of cigarettes on the table. "It's not like this is your first time in a police precinct. Juvenile records are sealed for some, but not all. As always, it's who you know."

Okay, so much for playing the innocent tourist. All the impatience, anger, and frustration I'd been bottling up over the last hour escaped out of my careless lips. "You realize your little friend there has been shakin' down vendors, right?" I said, nodding toward the door Jorge had exited.

Nefasto lit his cigarette, inhaled, and blew a plume of smoke. The carcinogens wreathed his face. "That's what you say. Words of a juvenile delinquent." He examined the paperwork he was carrying. "Actually, it says here you're what, twenty-three? Which means you can do real time in a real jail now, yes? Speaking of which, Jorge claims you were disturbing the peace and when he tried to talk to you...you attacked him, unprompted."

I rolled my eyes. "Good story. Got any with elves?"

Nefasto smiled and nodded. "Maybe he was exaggerating."

"You think?"

"I didn't say that I completely believed him." His eyes briefly flickered toward the surveillance camera bolted in the corner of the ceiling. "Whatever your perceptions are of Cuba or our government...our police do not tolerate corruption. We're not perfect, but—"

"Does that mean I can go?" The chains of my handcuffs clinked against the table.

Nefasto jetted smoke from his nostrils and leaned forward. "You still assaulted an officer. But...I may be able to talk Jorge out of pressing charges. If you are straight with me. Why are you here, in my country?"

I blew a stray piece of dark hair out of my face. "I needed a vacation." I kept a steady gaze and forced my breath into a calm even pattern that didn't match my racing pulse. Things could get complicated if this cop started digging around.

"There is no record of your entrance, which means you snuck in here or used false identification. Both suggest something more than a vacation."

"Oh, come on." I shrugged. "I didn't feel like going through the hassle of getting it approved and didn't have the money to go through Europe."

Nefasto stared at me through the cigarette smoke with watery, hazel eyes. I stared back. I could vaguely hear the big silver watch on his wrist ticking as he bit a fingernail in concentration. His fingertips were yellowed from smoking and matched his discolored teeth.

He leaned in, eyes moving to different parts of my face, like a human CAT scan. He finally flicked ashes onto the floor and shooed them away with his foot. "I suppose what this comes down to is deciding whether you're telling the truth or whether you're a very good liar."

A tall, bald officer poked his shiny head into the room. "Someone has come for the prisoner."

Nefasto stood, nodding to the bald man to unhook me from the table. I wasn't sure if that meant he was done with questioning me or they were letting me go, but I bit my tongue and made a silent plea with my mouth to stay shut.

He led me down a brightly lit hallway and opened a large metal door, which gave a loud creak. The precinct lobby was on the other side. Its egg yolk colored walls were chipped and sparsely lit by fluorescent lights that flickered, trying desperately to stay on. Even the wanted posters on a rotted chalkboard looked like they were twenty years old. Nefasto signaled for me to wait in the doorway, but I craned my neck around the corner and immediately spotted Mitch.

He was sitting on a wooden bench against the wall that should have been replaced years ago. Andy must have told him what happened. Otherwise he'd still be waiting in that empty apartment for me to show.

As soon as he saw me and Nefasto, he jumped to his feet. He pulled a finger from his lips, his worried eyes searching mine for answers.

Nefasto scanned the lobby and took a long, hard drag off his cigarette before heading over. "Are you here for Ms. Kafee?"

"Yes sir," Mitch answered, wiping his hands nervously on his jeans. "I'm her brother."

Seeing Mitch must have sold my story because Nefasto seemed to relax a bit.

"No jodas! You are even younger than she is," he said, shaking his head. "My name is Nefasto Oliva, Officer in Charge."

Mitch reached out to shake his hand. "I think there's been a misunderstanding."

"Yes, I believe so. Normally the one that bails out the other is more reasonable, so please listen carefully. I'm prepared to offer your sister a courtesy and release her into your custody." Nefasto pulled at the end of his nose and scratched the mustache portion of his goatee. "She has brought to light a...situation that I'd like to handle internally. Off the record."

"That's great, thank you."

"I will release her under one condition. You both leave the country. Immediately." Nefasto dropped his cigarette on the floor and put it out with his foot, then picked it up and put it in his pocket. "I don't know why the two of you are here and, frankly, I don't care. I just want the problem gone. Do we understand each other?"

"Yes sir."

Nefasto motioned to the bald officer standing behind me to fully remove my cuffs and then turned back to Mitch. "Then we have an agreement? You and your sister disappear. Tonight."

Mitch gave a quick nod. "Yes."

Nefasto turned and leaned in close to me as he passed through the metal door. "Adiós, Ms. Kafee," he whispered, a disturbing smirk lifting the corners of his mouth.

The bald officer shoved me forward. "You're free to go."

Mitch's worried eyes darkened with anger. He shot me a look and stormed outside.

I followed him through the precinct door and a gust of cool air chilled my bare skin. The clouds above seemed dark and impossibly full. They raced above me, as if they'd seen something horrifying coming. I picked up my pace and headed toward Mitch who was nearly jogging. This was going to suck.

As Mitch sped through the parking lot, I finally caught up to him.

"Mitch, I'm sorry, okay?" I said, grabbing his shoulder.

Mitch whipped around. "Arrested? Are you kidding me? Screwing up is like a reflex with you."

"Can we just skip this whole dramatic scene? We don't have time for this right now."

And at that very moment, the dark clouds burst. There was no warning drizzle, just immediate downpour. The rain fell like gunfire, sheets of it pounded against my face. The parched ground seemed to open and suck up the water in gulps. A peal of thunder rocked the sky as Mitch looked at me.

"We don't have time?" he yelled, stunned. "I'm not the one who was just in jail. It's bad enough when it's just your emotional shrapnel we all get hit with. But this is different. We're talking about Dad's life."

"You know, you've been doing this for years now.

Acting like you're so put upon, that it's up to you to take care of poor old Dad."

Mitch rubbed a hand across his face to clear his eyes of rainwater. "Well, someone has to. You're supposed to be some trained expert, and you've done *nothing* but waste time."

"We wouldn't even be here if it weren't for me," I barked.

"What does it matter if we can't save him? What if he's already dead, Tara?"

My clothes were soaked and I could feel strips of my hair sticking to my cheeks. "You don't think I've thought of that—" I stopped myself, biting off the rest of my sentence.

Mitch stared at me and his face fell completely. "He's dead. Isn't he?"

Before I could answer, a van skidded to a halt behind us. The sliding door was thrown open. Jorge and a tall man with pale skin both aimed guns at our heads.

Jorge cocked his gun. "Get in."

Mitch glanced at me. I gave him a subtle nod, and we got inside. Jorge slipped behind us and kicked us both to the floor as his partner grinned like a leering jack-o-lantern.

"Make a peep and Rico and I will take turns shooting you," Jorge said, jumping into the back and closing the door behind him.

Rico slid his tall gangly frame behind the wheel of the car. He rubbed his forearm across a large, hooked nose and reached for the gearshift. He threw it in drive, but then, oddly, put it back in park. He repeated this twice more before finally driving away. As we turned onto the main road, legions of raindrops pelted the metal hood in a constant, rhythmic beat.

Jorge sat with bent knees, leaning against the back of the passenger seat. He kept a firm grip on his gun, which remained pointed at us.

I turned to Mitch, and terror dawned in his eyes, like twin moons coming over the horizon. And I understood it. This was bad, really bad. But I had trained for this. We just had to wait for our moment.

I adjusted myself, but kept quiet, focusing on the tearing rasp of Mitch's breath and the rising pulse of the storm. Jorge was going to die.

CHAPTER SIXTEEN

WE DROVE FOR LESS than ten minutes before the van climbed a steep hill. I looked out through a small, begrimed window in the back. We were in a barrio. A thousand homes punctured the side of this large hill. Most were made of wood; some were patched with cardboard and waste material. Each and every one of them had supporting wooden stilts to lift the homes up and level the floors off of the sloping hillside.

After a series of twists and turns, we finally lurched to a stop. I looked out the windshield and noticed the rain had stopped, though my heart continued to beat in a hurried rhythm. My eyes subtly scanned the van, but always came back to Jorge's gun, still aimed at my head.

Seconds slipped by, then minutes, as Rico bounced out of the car, ripped open the side door and dragged us into an abandoned, single-dwelling house. Each passing moment was an opportunity lost. The narrow margin for escape was closing in on me faster than I could think.

As Jorge threw us down, I gave a quick and desperate look around. The place was rancid, with dirty floors and crumbling plaster. It smelled like old milk. The roof leaked and black mold drew a drippy wavering line down each corner. A makeshift wooden bar sat in the back with empty beer bottles fanned around it. It looked like something out of a slasher movie where campers were slowly killed off.

Rico forced us both into a kneeling, hunched position, then secured us by metal wrist cuffs with chains bolted to the wooden floor. Around us, the rotting planks were stained crimson. Remnants of other unfortunate souls who were once in the same spot.

Think, Tara. Think.

Once secure, Rico joined Jorge in the next room, a small kitchen, to converse in private. They mumbled to themselves and periodically glanced our way. A peal of thunder rocked the sky. The house reverberated with it. After a few seconds, lightning flashed and the lone window outside briefly transformed into a mirror. For a split second, I saw my own crestfallen face.

Mitch turned to me with terror in his eyes. "They're going to kill us, aren't they?" he whispered. "I'm scared, Tara."

I felt like someone was squeezing all the blood from my heart. He was right. I wanted to reach out and hug him, but I didn't dare move. Instead, I sank with him, blaming myself for getting us here. All of my training, the years in service, what good were they? That wild, impulsive, uncontrollable side of me had sabotaged it all. Every bad decision, every selfish move I'd ever made played through my head like a movie. For a moment, I let it all bury me.

Because of me, we were going to die.

I set my jaw. "No," I answered him. "I won't let them kill us."

From beneath the shrapnel of my defeat, the stubbornness in me crawled out of the deep, like some kind of tormented monster. I refused to lose the only two people I'd ever cared about. Not without a fight.

"Yes..." Mitch answered as he slumped forward. "We're going to die in this shithole." The rain that pasted his hair to his skull drizzled down the nape of his neck.

I stiffened; there wasn't time for this. I couldn't let emotion muddle my plan of action. I needed to look for any possible way out. In Iraq I'd never actually been captured, but the possibility of it was always there, and I'd gone over what to do a thousand times.

The first step was to take in every inch of your surroundings and use any possible tools at your disposal. I glared at Mitch. He was the smartest person I knew. I needed to use him.

I leaned closer. "Stop sulking and be part of the solution. Look around. Look for anything that could help us."

"It's over..."

"Don't do it because I asked you to, do it for Dad."

Mitch relented as if I'd injected him with a tiny Vitamin B shot of hope. He looked around the room.

I did likewise, checking the exits, checking for weak parts of the floor and the metal chain I was secured to. I turned and spotted a rack of guns near the entrance. No way to get to it, but it could come in handy later. I looked behind me at the wooden bar against the far wall. It could be used as cover. I glanced outside. To the right and left, the ground was level. Through the window behind me, the ground dropped off dramatically. The entire back portion of the house must have been held on stilt beams like the others on the block.

"This may be nothing," Mitch said suddenly.

I whipped around. "Tell me."

"The tall guy, Rico. He had to put the car in park and drive three times."

"I noticed that too. So?" I kept my eyes forward and my voice low.

"I think he has O.C.D."

"You mean, like, he's gotta turn the lights on and off before he leaves a room?"

"Exactly. I used to have this thing with the stove." He shook his head. "Doesn't matter, the point is that people who suffer from this type of OCD have rituals, normally relating to numbers. Repetitive behaviors they have to do a certain number of times. Rico's ritual is to repeat things three times. He couldn't drive, couldn't get out of the van till he put the car in park three times—"

Jorge suddenly turned, jabbed his gun and shouted from the kitchen. "Shut up. No more talk or I shoot you both right now."

As Jorge turned back, I waited a moment, then whispered to Mitch. "Anything else?"

"The floor. The wood is old and the blood may have softened it."

"Good. Yes. See if it has any play."

With this, both of us tested the wood.

"I've got nothing, you?" Mitch asked.

"Maybe," I nodded, straining. "I think so."

I almost had one bolt free. The previous pools of blood had weakened the wood. I rocked the bolt back and forth until the wood expanded around it enough to release it.

Before I could try the other bolt, Jorge and Rico came back in with a laptop computer. They set it on the table in front of us. Jorge tapped a few buttons, and after a moment Castillo's pockmarked face appeared on the video screen.

I stared at him. He leaned back and attempted the patrician look that must have served the male members of his family for generations. Only Castillo couldn't quite pull it off. It seemed forced, contrived. But there was also something in his eyes that reminded me to not take the man lightly. Something evil. My arms rashed out in goosebumps.

Castillo stared back at us for a bit longer, then adjusted his glasses. "Tara and Mitch Kafee, children of Harry Kafee. Seems like trying to catch me is a family business, yes?"

"We help out when we can," I quipped, not wanting to show weakness.

"You two kids want to be Extractors, too? Is that it? You want to take me back to America?" he asked, his overly white veneer teeth flashing as he spoke. "But you see, that would be...kidnapping. Which is frowned upon in my country."

"You should probably call the police."

"But I already have, my dear." Castillo motioned and a man sat down beside him—Nefasto.

Anxiety bloomed in my chest. Andy was right. Castillo owned this city. Nefasto knew exactly who I was the moment he ran my prints. He let me go on purpose. Jorge was never the problem he wanted handled off the record. We were.

"Nefasto." I ignored the rising surge of panic. "I don't suppose you feel like...doing your job. You know? Arresting the bad guy?"

Nefasto slowly shook his head. "I don't think so."

I tried to compose myself, focusing on Castillo. "Look, my brother and I couldn't care less about you. All we want is our father back."

"You're the military dropout, yes?" Castillo asked and

nudged Nefasto. "Or no, wait. They kicked you out. All those years of being a juvenile delinquent must have given you problems with authority. Women in the states are so willful. You must be a grave disappointment to your father."

I glared through the computer, my lips set in a tight, angry line. I opened my mouth to come back at him, but closed it again, too shaken by the truth in his words. Instead, I looked away.

"Oh, Tara, don't be ashamed. The most important people in society are always artists, criminals, and revolutionaries." He wagged his finger. "Only by questioning values can you force change."

I returned my gaze. "That what you're doing?"

"Me? I am most certainly forcing change. You see, I make weapons. I make them smaller and I make them cheaper. What I do is give power to the people."

My knees began to ache against the wood floor. I shifted, but kept talking. It was the only thing keeping us alive. "There are probably better ways to help people."

"That's where you're wrong," Castillo said, taking off his glasses. "You know...sometimes I wear contact lenses, not often, but sometimes. And these contact lenses have *1 2 3* on the inside, so that I don't put them in backwards. And I used to ask myself, why *1 2 3*, not *a b c*? Why not symbols of some sort? And then it came to me. Because *1 2 3* is universal. It allows them to ship these contacts all around the world. That's what my guns are, universal. They mean the same to everyone. They are equalizers. And since the entire world is my market. I can reach everyone. I can help more people this way."

"All I got from that little speech was that you get to sell more guns." I couldn't help myself. "Which means, it's about money. Which makes you a whore."

Castillo's upper lip lifted unconsciously, like a dog's when it's angry. And then a pregnant moment of silence ensued. He quickly calmed himself and continued.

"I understand why this frightens your country. Why they want to put me away. You want everything for yourselves. You want to be number one. Always. The problem is, Americans are the status quo, about to become status epilepticus. You know what this means?"

Mitch immediately answered. "A condition where the brain is in a state of persistent seizure. Is that supposed to mean our empire is about to crumble?"

"Very good. You must be the smart one." Castillo cupped his chin and squinted. "But I bet you've always felt inferior to your sister. Yes? She probably seemed so cool and mysterious. And with your head always in a book, I'm guessing you felt...less than. I was the same way."

"Really?" Mitch asked sardonically.

"Yes, I was ashamed of my IQ. Ashamed to know all the right answers in class. Envious of the bigger, stronger boys around me. Until I realized one thing...the strong may take from the weak...but the smart always take from the strong."

Mitch stared at him, stone faced, though the tips of

his fingers shook and his lips were drained of color. "Are you done?"

"Right. Enough chitchat. Where are my manners? You've come all this way to see your father, yes? You should say hello."

My breath caught as Castillo leaned forward, tapped a button with his claw-like, deformed hand and the screen split into two windows. *Was he alive?* The main window minimized, allowing the rest of the screen to show a view of a dank cement prison cell. And chained to the wall sat Dad. Bloody and bruised.

On screen, a guard grabbed him, and I gave an involuntary lurch forward. He was forced closer to the camera. A pink line of drool fell from his cracked, swollen lips. He tried to blink and finally looked up.

"Dad," the whispered word slipped from my mouth.

When he saw us he lost it. His head dropped and he jerked forward. Using all his force to pull against the chains, his face turning red with rage, and he let out a guttural cry. After a moment, he looked back up at the screen.

"No..." Harry said, his voice cracking. "Let them go. They're just kids—"

A fist came into frame and crushed Dad's jaw, sending him to the ground. I averted my eyes, unable to watch.

"Dad!" Mitch called out. He reflexively moved forward, but the chains on his wrists snapped and held him back.

When I turned back, Dad struggled to look up. "Leave

them alone. If you hurt either of my kids, I—"

Then with a flicker, the section of screen with Dad went blank, and the entire computer filled with Castillo's smug face.

"Get him back, put him back on screen!" I pleaded.

"I don't think so, it's better this way. Well, for me anyway. Imagination is always more powerful than reality," Castillo said slowly. "Your father, who has been tight lipped up until now, will wonder what we will do to his children if he doesn't show a little more cooperation."

"You piece of shit," I said, grinding my teeth.

Castillo clucked his tongue disapprovingly. "Such a mouth on such a pretty young girl. You know...I would have liked to spend a little alone time with you if things were different."

"Trust me. There's nothing more I'd like to do than get you alone."

Castillo's lips split into a devious smile. "We might be talking about two different things."

"Were you talking about me crushing your windpipe with my heel?"

Castillo's smiled evaporated. "Right, well, unfortunately, this is all the use I have for you two. So, you may now go with God."

With this, the screen went completely blank. A surge of adrenaline flushed through my veins. Time was running out. Whatever Jorge and Rico had planned, it was about to happen.

CHAPTER SEVENTEEN

I WORKED MY WRIST-CHAINS slowly and quietly but with maximum pressure. One bolt was free and the second was close. I subtly rocked it back and forth, the metal cuffs digging into my skin like dull knives. The wood was giving, but not fast enough.

In front of me, Jorge slapped the computer closed. He grabbed a leather roll and flipped it open. Inside were rows of silver knives. All shapes and sizes. They sparkled and shined. He held one in the air and ran his finger gingerly along the serrated edge, then tapped the tip like an exclamation point.

Time seemed to slow down. I heard the rain again, not just as a dull background thump, but really heard it—the manic, wild thrashing of the storm. It beat furiously on the windows and on the roof, almost in time with my heart. I glared at Jorge as he turned toward me, suddenly finding it hard to swallow.

"I like knives," he said. "Some people like guns, I prefer knives. It's more personal. More intimate. However, to do it right, rule number one is...you must tenderize the meat first." He grabbed a pair of brass knuckles and slipped them on. "That's why I have these."

"Yes, do it..." Rico said. The hook-nosed man swayed in place, a huge smile spreading across his face. He was clearly getting off on the whole thing as he rubbed his hands together and widened his eyes.

Jorge turned to Mitch. "You, being younger, and seeing as you haven't annoyed me...I will show mercy. It will be quick. I will open your carotid artery and you'll bleed out in less than five minutes."

"Yes, yes..." Rico said. He giggled and moved closer to get a better look.

Jorge turned to me. "You...I'm going to take my time with."

As he stepped closer, my gaze flickered to Mitch who noticed I had one hand entirely free. He glanced up at me realizing I still needed more time for the other.

"How's it feel?" Mitch blurted out.

Jorge turned back to him, squinting. "What?"

"To be a slave to a scumbag like Castillo instead of having the balls to step out on your own?"

"Ai Carrico, kid! I take back what I just said."

Mitch saw me desperately rocking the bolt on my other hand. He cleared his throat and continued. "Collecting scraps like a pigeon. Preying on people trying to earn a living—"

I watched in horror as Jorge staggered Mitch with a right hook. The brass knuckles split his lip.

"Stop it!" I cried out, my hands bunching into helpless, despairing fists. But then I went quiet, stunned by Mitch's reaction to the punch.

He didn't cry, he didn't whimper. He didn't even seem to be scared. Instead, he shook his head and smiled. He pressed his tongue to the gash inside his lip, almost impressed with himself, then spit blood back in Jorge's face. "You couldn't even do that right. Loser."

Jorge went psychopathic with anger. Rage fumed from his body like heat as he grabbed Mitch by the throat. So consumed, Jorge didn't see me free my second hand. I rose up, kicked Rico backward, then wrapped the chain around Jorge's neck, positioning myself behind him.

Jorge managed to retrieve the gun from his waistband, but I pulled the chain, yanked him close and trapped the gun with my free hand. We struggled for leverage, but I managed to turn the gun toward Jorge's chest, ensuring I was out of the bullet path. When it discharged he went slack, dropping with a thud. I let go of the chain and unwrapped if from his neck as blood pooled beneath his body, seeping into the cracks of the already stained wood.

I spun and saw the gun Jorge had dropped still skittering across the room. Only as I rushed for it, Rico stepped in between, his own gun aimed. He flicked his safety three times and was about to pull the trigger.

"That's four!" I cried out. "Your safety. Four times, not three."

Rico bit his lips, wanted desperately to shoot, but couldn't. As he quickly tried to perform his O.C.D. ritual correctly, I was on him. In one quick movement, I twisted the gun away and pivoted with a hammer-strike to his face. His nose caved like wet clay. Before Rico could cry out, I finished him with a left cross that sprayed teeth. He dropped to the ground like clothes falling off a hanger.

"Holy..." Mitch said, both stunned and impressed.

I ignored him and rifled through Rico's pockets. After finding the keys, I unlocked my metal cuffs, then ran to Mitch. His face was the bloody mess Jorge had meant for me.

"It's gonna be okay," I said as I freed him. Then I headed back to Rico. He was barely lucid as I jammed his own gun against his head.

"Where's Castillo?" I asked.

Rico could barely speak. His nasal cavities filled with blood. "I...don't know. I'm too lowly, I've never even met him in person."

I cocked the gun and a bullet filled the chamber. "Then you're no use to us."

"Wait, wait. Please."

"I'm gonna put this in terms you can understand. You've got *three* seconds to give me somethin' useful or you're dead. One..."

"Okay, okay. I...I know where you can find Nefasto. I don't know where Castillo is, but Nefasto does. Only he knows Castillo's location."

"Then where's Nefasto? Two seconds."

"He is supervising a delivery," Rico answered in a desperate rush.

"Weapons?"

"Yes, Castillo's latest batch."

I ignored how violently Rico was shaking. "How's it work?"

"The customer docks the boat, they exchange payment and load the boat. That's it. The boat leaves with the weapons."

"What dock, what time? One second."

Rico closed his eyes, and answered with a whimper. "Puerto de El Cochinito. Just before dawn."

I lowered the weapon, but as I shoved the man back, Mitch stepped up, pointing Jorge's gun at Rico.

"What are you doing?" I asked.

"Think about it. That weapons deal is the only thing we have left to go on. The only thing that might lead us to Dad. They can't know we're coming."

"What are you saying?"

"I'm saying, we can't risk him talking." Mitch leveled his gun at Rico, but I shoved it down.

"Just hold up a sec."

I stared at Mitch who gripped the gun tight. The sight was so completely disconcerting, it took me a moment to process. But this was the situation we found ourselves in. Standing in a rundown barrio shack with a man dead on the ground at our feet. Whatever innocence I hoped my little brother would hold onto was long gone. I'd seen a lot of guys only a couple years older getting shot and killed in combat. Boys in the second World War as young as thirteen were forging documents to join the fight. But this was different. This was my little brother.

A barrage of chronological images flicked through my head, Mitch as a five-year-old, dressed as a Power Ranger, then at ten, building a fort in the backyard, then again at fifteen with his learner's permit, almost driving into the neighbor's fence.

Mitch jabbed the gun at Rico. "He'll warn Nefasto that we're coming. I have to do this, right? Dad's life or his. I have to..."

"No," I yelled as Mitch fingered the trigger.

He paused and we locked eyes. Everything he'd said was true, but I couldn't let him do it.

Instead, I turned and fired myself, pulling the trigger without a second thought. The bullet struck Rico in the head, killing him instantly. He stayed upright for a split second, then accordioned in on himself, wavering like a shimmer of heat before dropping to the ground. I stared at the gun, a tendril of smoke curling around the barrel. My stomach sank with the sick feeling that only comes from taking a life, but I quickly swallowed down any hint of remorse and looked away.

"We need to go," I said.

Mitch stood stone-faced and stunned, but I headed for the door, pausing by the rack of weapons I'd noticed earlier. There were several types of rifles, but my hand jumped to a Remington 870 shotgun with a pistol grip. It had been sawed-off to a 12-inch barrel. I handed it to Mitch. "Hold this for a sec."

As I turned back to search through the rack, I heard something. Car doors closing, low voices, the shuffle of feet. I eased the door open just a crack, and less than fifty yards away, a phalanx of Castillo's men descended on the house like starving birds, pecking and fluttering, breaking formation and then gathering again. My heart caught as one of the men spotted me. He shouted something indiscernible and suddenly, a mad dance of lead ensued.

I slammed the door and threw down the lock bar. "Get down!" I yelled, grabbing another sawed off Remington and dragging Mitch to the floor.

Gunfire detonated around us as the men unloaded automatic weapons. When the shooting let up, I could see them through the windows flanking the sides of the house. I fired a few rounds to the right to slow them, grabbed a backup rifle, and pulled Mitch to the other end of the room, behind the wooden bar. As we waited, my heart ticked like a clock, keeping me present and alert to every sound, every movement.

"We're surrounded," Mitch said, clutching his gun like a security blanket.

I adjusted it and gave him a wide-eyed look forcing him to focus. "Point and shoot. Don't hesitate." Survival trumped preserving his innocence.

Mitch glanced down at the space between the wooden floor slats. There were two silhouette shadows moving. "Two more below."

I fired the shotgun down as the thugs underneath unloaded automatic weapons upwards. The dual blasts immediately disintegrated a large section of the floor, but I took out both men.

Mitch fired through the resulting hole a second too late, but struck a supporting beam stilt that held the structure up off of the hill. The wood ruptured and snapped, causing the entire house to drop down. It teetered at nearly the same angle as the hill. The remaining supports below held, causing the floor to bend. The two of us stumbled backward as the sides of the house split at the base and wood exploded in a perfect horizontal line. It rocked back and forth twice, but finally held.

Suddenly, the front door splintered off its hinges and more of Castillo's men boiled inside, MP5-Ks in hand. Before Mitch could regain his balance, I was back on my feet, gripping my shotgun. I took out several of the men, but a wave of bullets forced me into the kitchen.

Fear followed me into the small space, tightening my chest and slicking my palms with sweat. But over the years I'd learned to make her my friend. She'd never failed to keep me alive, to quicken my feet and sharpen my senses.

Tossing the empty gun aside, I reached for my rifle. The men lit up like targets in a shooting gallery. Using the wall as cover, I fired twice, dropping two as bullets shattered their knees. I fired more rounds into a third man, hitting his gut and shoulder. Another three men through the door were down, but this only bought me the split seconds I needed to get back to Mitch and take cover once again behind the thick wooden bar.

For a moment, I froze, my brain transporting me back to Iraq. To the firefights, the explosions and raining dust. As sweat dripped down my neck I remembered the way Fallujah seemed buried in heat and dirt—a city swallowed by the desert. Every crumbled building looked like this, abandoned and cluttered with debris. My eyes glazed over as I looked at the bloody mess of bodies on the floor and saw the squalid streets of Fallujah, littered with death. In a blink, Mitch became Dobbs, alive again, screaming for me to take cover.

"Tara!" he shook my shoulder and things blinked back to the present.

People were trying to kill us. They'd captured, tied up and tortured our father. These men and their allegiance to Castillo were responsible for killing an untold number of innocent people. Iraq was in the past. I forced myself to focus on the task at hand: survival.

"We're trapped," I said, looking around, thinking through scenarios and angles. "And I'm almost out of ammo."

As Mitch started to respond, a hailstorm of bullets raked the interior all around us. More men flooded inside and even more surrounded the house. I lifted my gun above the wooden bar and blind-fired to keep the men at bay.

Mitch breathed hard next to me; his hands shook at his sides as if infused with static electricity. The smell of burnt powder hung hot and savage in the air. "We can't shoot our way out of this, can we?" he asked.

The men yelled something in Spanish and I blind-fired again.

"No. Time to put that big brain to work."

Mitch was way ahead of me. He turned and stared at the floor, measuring something in his head.

"Maybe..." he said, squinting.

"Maybe what? What are you—"

Mitch aimed his shotgun and discharged into the floor. The blast took out another huge chunk and revealed the remaining large wooden stilt that held up the house. He turned to me. "That should be the last load-bearing beam."

"Okay, but what's that mean exactly?" I asked, ducking as another wave of bullets streamed overhead.

"It means...hang on." Mitch fired on the last beam. It fragmented, separated and the entire structure snapped from its supports. I braced myself against the wooden bar as the whole house ripped completely free. With an enormous crackle and groan it broke away and slid down the grassy hillside behind us. The house gained speed and plowed through every obstacle in its way. My fingernails clawed at the bar as we hit a cement partition, sending shattered shards of wood in all directions. I screamed as a telephone pole exploded through the middle of the wall, taking out several thugs, passing within inches of us and splitting the entire house in two.

One side pinwheeled laterally and careened into another barrio house, slicing it like a buzz saw. Which left us on the remaining half, sliding down the hill. I hung on with a white-knuckled grip and spun around to see we were fifty yards from the edge of the cliff.

Tossing my weapon, I lurched forward and grabbed a hold of Mitch with both hands. Just as the house was about to go over the side of the mountain, I leapt out, yanking Mitch with me. We hit hard onto the grassy knoll and slid, our momentum carrying us right to the edge, rolling, tumbling, before we finally straightened out and ground to a halt. We both looked up in time to see the last section of the house and all the remaining thugs inside, drop over the cliff. It arced slowly as it plummeted and finally disintegrated onto the rocky vista below.

I dragged Mitch to his feet and we looked at each other. I was sure his shocked, wide eyes mirrored my own, but after a moment he laughed and pulled me into an unexpected bear hug.

I smiled and hugged him back, the relief still washing over me.

"Holy...*shit!*" Mitch said, but I hushed him.

"We need to go. Before anyone sees us and realizes we didn't go over that cliff."

CHAPTER EIGHTEEN

I SAT ON THE couch in the safehouse, letting out a deep breath. Every inch of my body ached. My tattered jean shorts and T-shirt were covered in dirt and stained with blood. Miraculously, we'd made our way back here without incident, even after Mitch's cell phone died and we had to navigate based on familiar landmarks. Anyone else would need sleep, a bath, a meal. But all I could think about was the next step. Urgency sat trapped in my chest like a penned wolf.

"I'm going to check the bathroom for a first aid kit," Mitch said from the hallway.

I closed my eyes and rested my head against the worn sofa cushion. "I think I saw one in the medicine cabinet."

After a few minutes of rummaging, he stepped back into the living room. "Here." He threw a red zip-up bag onto my lap. "I got what I needed."

"Thanks."

I opened it and began dabbing peroxide on a myriad of abrasions up and down my legs and arms, then glanced outside. The sky was draining quickly, the horizon just a cuticle of pink. Mitch stopped at the sink to fill an enormous glass of water, then sat down at the tiny dining room table, his posture rigid and tense.

I finally broke the silence. "We have about ten hours till dawn. That's when the deal goes down. Given the nature of the transaction, we can assume Nefasto will have a lot of men there. Which means we won't have the firepower to take 'em head on. On top of that, we need Nefasto alive so we can, somehow, get him to tell us where Castillo is."

I waited for a response but didn't get one.

"If Nefasto's vehicle is a standard police car, we won't have the armor issue," I continued. "We can't just wing it, though. I need you to help me come up with a plan."

I stared at Mitch who downed his water in silence and wouldn't look up. As he got to the bottom, he tilted the cup vertical, catching the last few drops, then went right back to the sink and poured another glass.

I held my arms out. "Well?"

Mitch sat back down at the table. "Well what?"

I shrugged. "Would be nice if you helped me talk this through."

"It doesn't matter," he murmured.

The room felt swollen with humidity, and I swept the

hair off my neck. "What do you mean it doesn't matter? This is our last shot."

"Dad thinks Castillo has us. How long will he be able to hold out when they're threatening our lives? And once he talks, they'll kill him."

"We still have to try." I rubbed the back of my arms, trying to shake the anxiety creeping along the surface of my skin. "I took a lot of lives today so we could. I'm not backing down now."

"I just don't know how we can go up against another mob of his guys and not lose."

"You're right. But we don't have to do that. The Tiger, remember. We just have to get Nefasto alone. If we can get him to give up Castillo's location—"

"Sure. In theory. But we'll die trying."

"Maybe," I answered. But I'd come to terms with that possibility more times than I could count, with a lot less at stake than there was now. "You don't have to come."

Mitch kept quiet for a second. "I can't let you go alone."

Silence hummed between us.

"All of this still feels like a bad dream," he said. "I mean, a few weeks ago we were installing drywall in our backyard. How is the really happening?" He looked up at me, as if I had the answers. "Did you have any idea?"

My mind shuffled through past memories. There were subtle signs, but none of them obvious. Dad joined the Army when he was eighteen. Then, unlike me, he'd actually had a successful career in special forces after that. He kept a gun safe next to the bed and knew his way around a pistol. He'd taught me how to load and fire one at the shooting range, and instead of signing me up for dance, he spent an hour a week teaching me self-defense when I was thirteen. I'd always just assumed it was his way of bonding with me after Mom left. I'd chalked it all up to him not knowing how to relate to a girl.

As I got older there were other things that seemed odd. He was overly obsessed with his military background. He kept disarmed bombs in our garage along with a strange collection of "retired" military weapons as souvenirs. Our bookshelves were decorated with inactive grenades and RPGs. He'd regularly traveled for work, but back then it seemed normal. Manufacturers were overseas. Then there was the time I stayed home sick and he had to stop by work. He'd made me wait in the car because special security clearance was needed to get inside. At the time I didn't question it. Though I couldn't imagine other appliance companies requiring any kind of security clearance to enter the building.

But that was Dad. Most of the time he cooked and kept the house organized, did crosswords and watched the news. Just like any other single parent.

"No," I finally answered. "I mean, it makes sense now, looking back, but I had no idea."

"Me either. It's so...I just can't imagine him killing people. I feel like our whole life was a lie. I didn't even know him."

"It wasn't a lie. He's still Dad. He still loves us. That's the reason he kept it all from us."

Mitch bit his cheek and gazed into the surface of the table. "So, what's your plan again?" he asked.

"Get Nefasto alone. Force him to tell us where Dad is or Castillo."

"Yeah, but Castillo's guys will be armed, including Nefasto. We don't know how many guys will be there or what the environment will be like. It could be hard to isolate and grab him."

The subtle drone of a car driving by outside tempered the quiet room as I thought.

"What if we let the deal go down and follow Nefasto until he's alone?"

"I like it," Mitch said. "But...he's a cop, won't he be good at spotting a tail? We lose him, we're screwed."

I nodded, trying to come up with something else.

Mitch's eyes ticked back and forth, as if all the variables were spinning like a roulette wheel inside his head. Finally, he pulled out his iPhone. "It's got GPS and a tracking app. We put this in his car and we don't have to physically track him at all."

"That could work," I brightened, actually hopeful. "But isn't it dead?"

Mitch smiled. "The first thing I bought when we went shopping for the club was a phone charger." He stood and pulled it from an outlet behind the couch. "We also need to pinpoint the location of the deal," he said, plugging it in.

I leaned forward, resting my forearms on my bare thighs. "Maybe if we use Google maps we can zoom in and figure out what the dock looks like."

"You think we should ask Andy if he knows anything about the location that might help us?"

Andy. I shot to my feet, pinning my hair back with my hands. "Shoot!"

"What?" Mitch asked.

"Jorge arrested me at Andy's shack. If he told Nefasto about seeing us together, they'll figure out he was Dad's contact."

Mitch's mouth hung open for a brief moment as he connected the dots.

My heart beat faster. "I have to warn him."

Grabbing a few bills from our roll of cash and the drug dealer's gun from the kitchen drawer, I headed for the door, but stopped with my hand on the knob.

"What?" Mitch asked.

"I need you to write down your phone number," I said, searching the kitchen for a pen and paper.

"Why?"

"I don't have it memorized, and I don't have my phone. They confiscated it from me at the police station. Write it down just in case things go wrong."

"I'll just go with you."

"No. I'll be fine, and I can move faster alone. Just stay

here. No anxiety running or whatever." He scribbled it down and gave me a worried look as I headed out. "Try to sleep and eat something," I said over my shoulder.

Out on the busy street I stashed Mitch's number in my back pocket and looked around for a place to buy food. The café from this morning seemed like my best bet. Eyes followed me as I made my way to the counter, and paranoia set in. Any one of them could rat me out to Castillo. I looked like a feral cat who'd just lost a fight. It was pretty obvious something was wrong.

I tapped my hand on the wooden table in time with my rapid pulse, willing them to hurry, and nearly ripped the burrito from the young server's hand when it was done.

Heading down the sidewalk, I devoured oversized bites, trying to finish quickly. At this point, even eating was an annoying obstacle in my way. As I walked, the road ahead seemed so long. Everything felt too far out of my control. If Andy was okay, maybe he could help me think it all through. He knew the place better than I did.

Although the sun had set, the heat felt unrelenting. I wiped at my brow with the hem of my T-shirt as the light above me brightened and faded with each passing streetlamp. Soon, the city nightlife came alive, slowly becoming a cacophony of distant dance music, traffic sounds, and mulling crowds mixed together as I headed toward the beach.

Once Andy's shack came into view, guilt pooled in my

gut like a bullet wound. What if they'd already gotten to him? I should have pushed him away a long time ago. But the truth was, I was glad he'd helped us, and secretly I hoped he still would.

I scanned the coast. With a wave of relief, I spotted Andy on the mostly empty beach, packing up gear and loading it into a beat-up jeep. He closed up the back and slid behind the wheel.

"Hey," I called before he could drive away.

Andy turned, defensive at first, but the moment he saw it was me his posture changed, and his features lightened with surprise.

"You..." His dark eyebrows and large lips lifted.

I stepped closer as he got out of the car. "Sorry, I didn't mean to pop out of nowhere," I said. "I was so worried."

Andy reflexively hugged me, which caught me off guard, but after a moment I let myself relax into his chest, thankful for the brief moment of comfort.

Toasted-coconut-scented sunscreen floated from his T-shirt as he pulled away. "I didn't know if..." His words came spilling out in a quick burst. "I saw him, Jorge...and the van. I was waiting in the parking lot. I didn't know if my being there would make it worse for you. Some of those guys work for Castillo. I was too late. I thought if I stayed at my hut, Jorge would come back for me, and I could..." His eyes found the scrapes and cuts I'd earned in the last few hours, taking in the state of my blood-spattered clothing, and his thumb gently brushed a gash on my shoulder. "Did he hurt you?"

"He's dead."

Andy let out a breathy laugh, but then realized I wasn't joking. "Did you kill him?"

I shrugged. "It was him or us."

He nodded his head too many times.

"Okay. Yeah. Okay," he said, his cinched eyebrows revealing the depth of his concern. "Um...let me put this stuff away and I'll drive you to the apartment. You should rest."

I hopped into the passenger side without arguing.

"Is Mitch okay?" he asked.

"Yeah. He's at the safehouse."

"Good."

He started the jeep and drove through traffic for a few minutes, then down an alley between two large concrete buildings. As he reached the end, he stopped in front of a storage garage.

"Listen," I said, before he opened the door. I took a deep breath, summoning the courage to confess a reality that would very likely ruin his life. "There was a guy at the station named Nefasto. He works for Castillo, and he figured out who I was the minute he ran my prints." Andy nodded at the grim truth as if he'd expected it. "Jorge is dead, but we don't know if he told Nefasto he found me with you. If he did, it's only a matter of time before they figure out you were my Dad's contact. It isn't safe for you to be out here."

He surveyed the alley, and his eyes flickered to the rearview. "You're probably right. But I've been waiting for this day. They've been toying with me long before I met you. It's not your fault."

He got out of the car and fumbled with a set of keys, then opened the storage unit.

"What do you mean, they've been toying with you?"

"Castillo and I have a history. Jorge was his man. They've been making my life hell for years, which is one of the reasons I was hoping to get out of the country. But he's not exactly a guy you run from unless you have a way to cover your ass. He's a weapons dealer. He knows people who can kill you all over the world, no matter where you go. I figured the CIA could help me out with that, which is why I volunteered to help your Dad."

He flipped on the lights and I followed him through the door of his storage unit. Inside, it was filled with all of the equipment for his excursions: Zip-line gear, kayaks, scuba tanks, and diving gear.

He grabbed a large duffle bag from the corner, neglecting to unload the gear in the jeep, and threw it into the backseat.

"Why didn't you tell me any of this?" I asked.

"I told you I had my reasons for helping you." He glanced at the bag he just threw into the car. "If they're really looking for me, I have a place I was planning on hiding out. Let me take you and Mitch—"

"We can't. I just wanted to make sure you were safe

and knew you could be in danger."

"Tara." He stepped closer, and I felt myself tense up as he reached for my hand. "If you really did kill Jorge...you know they'll be looking for you. They know who you are now, what you look like." He must have surprised himself, because he glanced down at our touching fingertips and seemed hypnotized by the contact. "You need a truly safe place to hide out. Showing your face in this city is risky. Even if you stay near the safehouse. You don't know who you can trust."

"Okay," I answered immediately. "If it's not far, you can show me, then we can meet you there later if we need to."

He looked at me with deep concern and squeezed my hand. "Why? What's later?"

"We have a lead on one of Castillo's weapons deals. We're hoping one of his guys will lead us to him."

Nervous energy reverberated between us and I let my fingers drop. There was no way to know what the next twenty-four hours would bring.

"How much time do you have?" he asked.

"Mitch and I need to be at the docks at dawn..."

As he looked up, the thought of kissing him was reckless and selfish, but I couldn't pull my eyes from his lips.

Andy cleared his throat. "Then we should hurry." He gestured to some scuba gear against the wall and turned to pick it up. "Do you know how to dive?"

CHAPTER NINETEEN

AFTER USING ANDY'S PHONE to send a quick text to Mitch explaining the plan, the two of us jumped into his jeep and headed back toward the beach. He parked alongside a dirt road and we carried scuba equipment to a rickety wooden dock near a large cement slab cluttered with ghostly vehicles left to rust. Tied to the pier, several aluminum fishing boats with old outboard motors swayed and tugged against their ropes.

"Is this place underwater?" I asked as he helped me gear up with the proper scuba equipment.

"No. It's just hard to get to. For a reason."

Neither of us bothered with wetsuits, but the air tanks, masks and regulators were nonnegotiable. I pulled the large fish-bowl goggles over my eyes and nose.

"Okay, is that it?" I asked, my voice muffled and nasally. "If Mitch and I need to do this without you, I want to make sure I know what I'm doing."

Andy couldn't hold in his laughter.

"Yes." He fitted his mask to his face causing his upper lip to stick out like a duck pout. "But we don't have to wear the masks yet."

I smiled and lifted it off my face. "Is there more equipment at the storage unit if we need it?"

He pulled his mask up too. "Yes, but I'll leave your stuff in the boat when we're done."

Once we were ready, Andy led me onto a large beat-up speedboat with faded green fabric seating. He pushed us off, cranked up the motor and headed out to sea. With all that had happened I couldn't help but appreciate the simple brush of wind on my skin or the way the dark water shimmered with gold flakes of moonlight. Warm air threw back the loose pieces of my hair and whipped gently at my clothes as I watched the shoreline, committing the route to memory.

Less than half a mile down the coast and a hundred yards from shore, Andy dropped a small anchor. He unlocked a storage compartment and dragged out two Underwater Sea Scooters. They were bright yellow, and a little over two feet long, resembling a fan with two handles. But, as I'd learned in the service, these things generated enough thrust to pull a body underwater at nearly five mph.

"Nice," I said, impressed.

"And not cheap. Let me show you how to operate—"

"It's okay. We used them for dive training."

"Dive training?"

I almost forgot how little he knew about me.

"I was in the Marines." I lifted up the short sleeve of my shirt revealing my tattoo. "Special forces…"

His eyebrows shot up. "You're in the Marines?"

"I *was* in the Marines," I corrected.

"Makes sense." He smirked. "You're not like most girls."

I narrowed my eyes at him, trying to decide if he meant it as a compliment.

"In a good way," he clarified. "I like that you don't let anyone push you around."

"Thanks."

Andy slipped on his scuba tank and helped me with mine.

"Okay, come on." He hooked a waterproof bag of supplies from his duffle to the handle of one of the Sea Scooters and dropped both of them in the water. "Stay close and follow me."

After pulling down his mask, he popped in his ventilator and jumped overboard. I did the same, the cool water making my muscles tense up at first. Soon it became comfortably tepid and I found Andy, who pushed one of the Sea Scooters toward me. He grabbed his, and as he twisted the throttle, it yanked him forward. I flicked on the Scooter's headlamp and gunned it, following the wake of bubbles he left behind.

As we glided through the clear cool water, a group of silver fish materialized out of the dark blue limbo. They spread open and allowed us through. Andy pointed his Sea Scooter down, coasting close to the bottom, and I followed suit.

My headlamp swept past a large coral reef, and I took a moment to soak it in. It looked like a giant rainbow cloud of rock. Each cluster seemed to be a different color, bright blues, reds, yellows and greens.

After a few minutes, the shore became visible ahead. It was a clear horizontal line, except for one section where a small ocean inlet cut away the ocean floor, forming a river-like path. Andy led me toward it, and we passed through a cave-like opening. On the other side, shimmying above the water, a shadowed line of thick trees hovered over the inlet, like some ancient hidden passage.

Andy steered the propulsion device upward. I followed and quickly broke the surface, finding myself in a tiny lagoon, ringed with Mangrove trees. Their roots were a loosely tangled mess of sea snakes that reached for the water's edge and the branches above were so densely interlaced that only thin silver threads of moonlight seeped in, as if the fabric of the sky was unraveling directly into the lagoon.

Andy removed his mask and I lifted mine onto the top of my head like sunglasses. For a moment we bobbed in the water, the quiet lapping of subtle waves and our breath the only sound in the quiet space. Andy swam closer, his lips and face wet with seawater.

"Here," he said, guiding me to the edge with a hand on my hip. "I'll help you out."

I reached for a tree root and Andy hoisted me up onto the dirt. Once out, I turned and took Andy's hand, helping to pull him onto the lifted shore. It was treacherous and beautiful.

"Pretty amazing hideout," I admitted, squeezing water from my hair. Even in the warm tropical air, my wet clothes made me shiver.

"Come on." Andy unhooked his waterproof bag and took my hand. "I'll light a fire."

It was obvious he came here a lot. A small stone circle fire pit was already set up, the center filled with ashes. Tangled loose branches and thick broken logs sat clustered to the side along with a small black plastic container I assumed was for a lighter and other essentials.

I sat on the firm ground near the fire pit. "This is so—" my voice caught in my throat as Andy removed his wet shirt and threw it on a rock. "Cool..." I finished, noticing a scar that ran from his abdomen around the lower section of his back.

"How'd you get that?" I asked, forcing myself to look away.

Andy let out a breath and slipped into a fresh white T-shirt from the bag. "Castillo."

My eyebrows lifted in shock. When he'd said they had history, I didn't imagine it being so intimate. "I can see why you hate him." More questions lingered on my lips, but I chose not to ask, hoping he'd decide on his own to tell me what happened.

"He's an easy man to hate." Andy reached behind a large rock and pulled out another black duffle. "Here," he said, unzipping the bag and throwing me a faded blue T-shirt with palm trees on the front. "I've been bringing clothes and things here in case they come for me."

Guilt kept me quiet.

Without my needing to ask, he turned his back so I could change. I peeled off my wet shirt, slipping the soft dry cotton one over my damp body.

"So, what's your history with Castillo, anyway?" I asked, unable abate my curiosity. "You said they've been toying with you. Why?"

Andy collected dry tree roots and branches from his wood pile for the fire, taking a moment before he answered.

"When we met, I wasn't sure I could trust you. I lied about being denied a visa because my uncle defected. I never applied. Even if I did, they wouldn't give me one because," he shrugged, "I too have a criminal record." His eyes glinted with a sparkle of gold as he lit a small fire.

"Three years ago, I was working as a waiter at a hotel. Castillo ordered room service, and when I went to his room, I heard screaming. A girl." The subtle accented rhythm of his voice was hypnotic in the sound-dampened lagoon. "I used my hotel key, went inside and saw he was getting rough with her. I pushed him away, he pulled out a knife. I should've died, but Castillo lives to torture people. He had me seen to, made sure I lived, paid a witness to testify that I attacked him and it was self-defense. I was the one arrested. Once I was out he made sure I knew that I owed him and he's had Jorge shaking me down ever since, forcing me to be his...what do you call it...when you take stolen merchandise and sell it?"

"We call it a 'fence'."

"Yes, right." Andy nodded. "Castillo said if I ran, he'd find me, find my family, that I was his and he was doing me a favor by letting me run my business and stay alive. As my grandmother would say 'he's as evil as natural and physical as a hillside'."

Andy brushed his wet hair off his face. "Anyway, I have a second cousin in America who is married to an analyst in the CIA and when they reached out to me I felt like it was my only chance to get out. I want to take Castillo down as much as anyone."

"Wow." Our eyes connected over the small flames. "I had no idea. What about your family? Are they all still here in Cuba? Are they safe?"

Andy leaned toward the fire. "They all made it over to the states, legally, before any of this happened. Which means there's nothing I can do to protect them. They don't even know they're in danger if...." He stood to grab more wood, then tossed it on the flames sending a dancing spiral of sparks into the air. "So, what's your plan?" he asked, changing the subject. "To get your dad back?"

He sat down beside me, prodding the fire with a stick.

"Actually, I was hoping you could help me with that part," I admitted. "You know this place and these people better than I do."

The moon tried its best to break through the canopy of trees above us as we talked through scenarios and Andy drew maps in the dirt with his fingertips until I felt more confident in how to play it.

"It's our last chance," I said, looking up at him. He was so easy to talk to; so present. There was never any judgment in his eyes.

"You said you were in the Marines, so you've dealt with things like this before, yes?"

I shrugged. "I always had a team behind me. Higher ups giving orders. Honestly, I should be prepared, but it's my *dad.* I feel totally out of control. I've already messed everything up so much."

Andy nodded slowly, then looked up at me, the flames from the fire shadowing his face with delicate tones. "None of this is your fault," he said. "Whatever happens, your dad made choices that got him here, not you."

"It doesn't matter whose fault it is. I can't afford to screw up. I can't let him down again." I paused, dark thoughts dragging me under. "If he's even still alive...."

"Don't think like that." Andy reached for my bare knee, his touch warm against my chilled skin. I looked down at the fire, but he reached over and turned my chin toward him. "It will all work out."

We stared into each other, and I felt myself lean closer. His hand moved to my cheek as he moved in slowly. Before I could think it through his lips sank into mine, and I caved. I let it all come crashing in on me, whatever it was between us. He kissed me cautiously at first, a slow and gentle taste of temptation, but the rush took me over, my breath growing heavier as Andy's mouth slid to my neck.

My hand slipped under the hem of his shirt, and the feel of his skin made me pull back. This was wrong. I should be focused on my family.

"Sorry," I said. "With everything going on with my dad, everything that happened today..." I couldn't bring myself to finish. What was I trying to say anyway?

"I understand."

I looked away from him searching for a distraction. "So, uh..." I waved toward a small squadron of fireflies that floated in formation above me. "You guys have fireflies here?"

Andy laughed at my obvious attempt to lighten the mood. He nodded, caught one and held it toward me. Its rear end glowed brightly. "Alecton discoidalis. I had to do a paper on them once in school. They are some of the largest and most luminescent in the world."

The bug flew off and I smiled. "Good to know."

Andy moved closer. "Would it be terrible if I kissed you again?"

My cheeks immediately flushed hot. His dark eyes

held mine, intent, warm and unabashed. This was the worst possible time, but I was so tired of having to be tough, of trying to pretend that I had it all together. That everything would be okay. Right now, the only thing I wanted was to be held.

"No," I said tentatively. "It wouldn't be *terrible*."

Andy was already leaning in. My eyes closed as he pressed against me, and I melted underneath him, laying back on the dirt floor. His heart beat against mine and his hand swept against my waist as we kissed.

I gasped as he rolled and dragged me on top of him, but only let the small hesitation linger for a second before finding his lips again.

I could take things further. I wanted to. Instead, I pulled back, slid down and rested my head on his chest. His pulse was fast, and the warmth of his body radiated through me. I slid off and tucked myself into the crook of his arm, laying my head on his shoulder.

He hugged me, without trying to push for anything more, and I stared at the stars above, unwinking and constant. Maybe this is what life could be like when all of this was over. All those suns, worlds, dizzying constellations and galaxies by the millions made my problems feel small, if only for the briefest second. And for the first time in close to a decade, I let go.

No more being closed off and numb. All my walls that continually needed repair exhausted me. No matter how I rationalized it, I felt something for Andy. It was rushed, under horrible circumstances and the timing couldn't possibly be worse. But I couldn't deny what I was feeling. So, I allowed myself this one small moment.

Andy squeezed me tight and kissed the top of my head. I closed my eyes, imagining I was home, pretending sleeping in his arms was a nightly comfort. And eventually I began to dream.

"WE SHOULD GO."

I jolted awake at the sound of Andy's voice, suddenly terrified I'd slept through the morning.

"What time is it?" I gasped, sitting up.

The fire had gone out, but thankfully the pieces of sky winking through the tangled branches of the lagoon were still a dark shade of purple.

"3:30," he answered.

My frenzied heart slowed and I let out a deep breath. There was still time.

"I wanted to let you sleep. I texted Mitch, but I think it's best we get going."

"Yeah."

As much as I wanted to push the truth away, I couldn't. I had to face the dawn and whatever came with it.

Without much to say, I got to my feet, the stark reality of what I had to do, a looming storm cloud in the distance.

BACK AT THE safehouse I found Mitch sitting on the balcony. The sliding screen door made a slight scraping sound as I opened it and stepped out. I plopped down in the rusted chair beside him, and for the next twenty seconds, we sat together in silence.

"About two hours until we leave," Mitch said, staring forward.

I nodded, dread sitting heavy in my stomach, and I couldn't think of a thing to say. In the distance, a large freeway split the city. I hadn't noticed before, but our building was on a small hill which provided quite a view from this direction. The city below was an enormous imbroglio of color, resisting the smothering cloak of night with its noise and light. Even when the sun was down, Havana refused to submit. I closed my eyes for a moment and soaked in the sounds, the occasional bleat of horns and the meshing gears of the giant mass of vehicles all concentrated into white noise.

Eventually I turned to Mitch. "How's your face?" I asked.

One side of his lip looked like a bad silicone implant. A spotted line of bruises dotted his left cheekbone, four perfectly round circles the size of shot glasses, compliments of Jorge's brass knuckles.

He moved his jaw around and winced. "I have this sound, like a distant hum, from behind my right ear. And the throbbing is going down my spine, all the way to my feet." His shoulders bobbed with a shrug. "Looking like a badass was one thing, feeling like one…sucks."

"Yeah." I laughed. "I'll get you some ice."

He held up a plastic bag, half melted from the table next to him. "I'll be fine."

I leaned back in my chair, glancing back through the sliding glass door at Andy who was checking his phone at the kitchen counter.

"I found this," Mitch finally said, lifting Dad's coat from the ground next to him.

He handed it to me. I took it and pressed it to my cheek, picking up on the faintest scent of home—a mix of sun-baked leather and Dad's cologne. If things didn't work out tonight, it might be the closest I ever got to him again.

"This was in the pocket," Mitch added, revealing a silver chain with a pendant on it he'd had clutched in his hand. He pulled down the collar of his shirt revealing a quick glimpse of his own chain. The very one he told me he no longer had.

I blinked up at the sky trying to stop the pooling tears. "You're such a liar," I teased him with a breathy laugh. "I knew you still had it."

Dad had bought the chains for the three of us after Mom left. Just like mine, the medallion on the end was of Saint Anne. She was the mother of the Virgin Mary and grandmother of Jesus Christ. She watched over families, kept them safe and together. That's what Dad had promised. That even though Mom was gone, he would never leave. That we'd always be a family together, no matter what.

I looked out at the distant ocean, and thought of her. I wondered where she was, what she was doing. Was she safe? Did she miss us? Would the fact that her husband's life was in danger matter to her? Would she care that Mitch and I had risked our lives to try and save him?

I remembered the day she left. It was just before my thirteenth birthday. We'd made plans to go to Disneyland the next day. Mom spent all night telling me all about it. The rides, the food, how much fun we would have.

I remembered her kissing me on the forehead before bed. How she turned out the lights, but left the door cracked, so a tiny bit of light could stream into the room. She hadn't acted strange; there was no sign that anything was wrong.

But the next morning, she was gone. No goodbye, just a note saying, *Take care of them.* After all I'd learned about Dad, I had to wonder. How much did she know? There was no way he could hide something like this from his own wife, could he? For the first time in years, I considered whether there was more to it than I'd thought. Something deeper. Maybe it wasn't her fault.

"You know," I said, "whatever happens with Dad..." I wasn't the best at this stuff, but I forced the rest out, because I needed him to know. "I'm not going anywhere. I'm staying with you. And I know you think I'm just some screw up who can't follow through, but...I'll be there Mitch. I promise."

He nodded, staying quiet at first, but I could tell he was letting down his guard. "Thanks," he said after a while. "But you don't have to. You're not Mom, and I know I've kind of pinned that on you."

I smiled, feeling his thick wall of resentment start to crumble. "Yeah, so our mom left. We've got issues. I get it."

"Can I ask you something?" He looked out at the twinkling lights of the city. "Why didn't you let me shoot that man? Rico. You made sure you pulled the trigger. Why?"

I didn't even need to think about it. I knew exactly why. "Because I know what it's like. It's one thing to shoot someone shooting at you. That's fight or flight, something you can rationalize. But to kill an unarmed man, even if he was trying to kill you five minutes earlier...that's different. It changes you. It takes something away from you. I guess...I wanted to protect you from that."

"I get that you want to protect me," Mitch said. "Maybe you don't want me to become...you. But, there's a theory in philosophy, the more you try to protect something, the more vulnerable you make it."

I nodded. "That...makes sense."

"It got me thinking. I can't depend on everyone else forever. I'm eighteen. Eventually I'm going to have to step out and do things on my own. Be a man. And to be honest, there's a huge part of me that actually likes the feel of a gun."

"You like it?"

"It's hard to explain. For some people, life is easy, but for me...it's a constant struggle, always has been. Every minute of every day, I'm consumed by anxiety. You know when you take a car out of gear and press the accelerator. That's my brain 24/7. I over-think everything. And it's exhausting," Mitch said, leaning back. "But when I shot that gun...even if just to take out the support beam, all of that vanished. My head was crystal clear and for the first time I can remember, I felt in control. Does that make any sense?"

"Yeah...it does."

Mitch pulled his necklace out from beneath his shirt and dropped the Saint Anne medallion onto his chest where I could see it. I smiled for a moment. The old Mitch, the chin-to-chest, stare at your shoes little brother he'd always been to me, had grown up while I'd been gone. I could almost see him becoming a man. And if there was anyone in the world I could trust when the bullets came flying, it was Mitch.

I locked eyes with him. "Let's get Dad back."

CHAPTER TWENTY

WITH ONLY TWO HOURS until sunrise, the three of us stood around the kitchen counter picking apart our most recent plan.

"But even if we plant the phone, he may not go straight to Castillo right after," Mitch added. "We can't assume Nefasto will lead us to him right away, and we might run out of time."

"What if we could force his hand somehow?" I asked, trying to solve the puzzle. "Do something to make him have to meet Castillo face to face. Make him lead us there without knowing it."

Andy looked at me. "What would make him do that?"

They probably weren't going to like my answer, but it could work. "This transaction has to go bad," I said. "Really bad."

JUST BEFORE DAWN, Andy drove us to Puerto de El Cochinito, a large commercial loading port on the edge of Cuba's coastline. The metal claws and posts that crowded the shore were worn by age, yet still functional. It was easy to imagine the buzz and hum of a busy workday, but tonight the industrial monster slept. Fifty or so forklifts lay dormant and several quiet cranes kept watch over a maelstrom of large metal shipping containers stacked on the docks like giant, multi-colored Lego bricks.

I sat quietly in the front seat of Andy's Jeep, trying and failing to figure out how to say goodbye to him. His help had been invaluable, but this was where it needed to end. I had decided on the drive over that this was our fight, not his. Despite his personal history with Castillo, I couldn't put *another* person I cared about at risk.

As he parked and shut off the car I turned to him. "Thank you…I—"

Andy threw the keys under the seat. "Let's go."

"Wait," I said, jumping out and trapping Mitch inside the car.

Mitch's voice muffled through the glass, but I ignored him.

My shoes crunched the gravelly road as I confronted Andy. "You can't come."

"What? Why?"

"Because this could go...badly."

"Exactly," he said, his dark eyes full of a new intensity I hadn't seen before. "That's why I'm coming. You said yourself you're outnumbered and outgunned. You need all the help you can get. You might be able to handle yourself, but what about Mitch, huh? He's a good kid, but come on. If things go bad, like you say, you need someone who won't hesitate."

I averted my eyes, already feeling guilty enough bringing my little brother. "Well, he won't stay in the car, I know him."

"All the more reason you need my help. Me keeping an eye on him frees you to do what's necessary, right?"

"I've already dragged you way too deep into this—"

"I told you. *You* didn't drag me into this. This day has been coming for a while. It's time for me to make my move." Andy opened the door to let Mitch out. "We don't have time to argue. It's my choice. Let's go."

My stomach turned at the thought of either of them getting hurt, but he was right. We didn't have time to argue.

Andy led us into the maze of shipping containers until we were close enough to the water we'd be able to see any boats in the area.

"We need to get higher," I whispered. "Find a vantage point." I scanned the yard and locked in on a stack of empty wooden crates. "There."

Mitch and Andy began stacking them against the wall

of one of the storage units until the crates were high enough to climb. I hoisted myself on top of the giant boxcar and army-crawled to the center. Mitch and Andy did the same, flanking my sides.

Lying stomach-down on top of the metal container, the air felt too warm, even this late at night. Sweat dripped from my temples as I waited. Mitch waved a hand at the gnats and mosquitoes that swam through the thick, humid air around us, and Andy wiped his brow for the fifth time in an hour.

Finally, I heard voices. Castillo's guys arrived fully armed as expected. Their casual Spanish conversation echoed around the dock as they hauled and placed several unmarked wooden crates against one of the containers.

As the sky began to lighten into a pale gray, I spotted the buyers. "There."

I nodded my head as three Stryker go-fast boats slid into a line and were tied to the wooden side dock. Their captains, three highly armed, light-haired men speaking something that sounded slightly German, jumped off the boats and greeted one of Castillo's guys.

"Austrians?" Mitch whispered

"Scandinavians, I think," I answered.

After a quick exchange, the light-haired men began loading up their newly acquired armory. I clocked the action below, watching as they opened the crates and the weapons inside were carefully transferred to secret compartments within the boats.

"Okay, so what exactly is your plan to make this deal go bad? I mean, specifically," Mitch asked.

"You plant the phone in Nefasto's car," I answered, "then, Andy and I rain on this little parade down there."

"That is infuriatingly vague."

"What if we stole one of the boats?" Andy asked. "After they're loaded with product."

"They lose product and more than that..." I said. "Castillo looks bad to his buyer."

Andy nodded. "That would most certainly call for a face-to-face explanation."

We all seemed to agree, so for the next several minutes we watched them work.

"This dock's like a freakin' drive-thru for weapons." Mitch looked around, then began to chew on his thumbnail. "But where's Nefasto? He's gotta show up to get the cash, right?"

I was asking myself the same question. What if he didn't show? What if we'd assumed wrong and this whole thing was a dead end? I didn't have a backup plan.

"Those blond guys aren't leaving until they pay up, trust me," Andy answered. "We just need to be patient."

The three of us waited in silence, until my bony joints started to ache against the metal roof. Mitch squirmed next to me, adjusting himself into a more comfortable position, crossing his arms and laying his cheek on his wrist.

He finally turned to me. "Hey, can I ask you something?" he whispered.

I nodded.

"Do you think Mom knew? About Dad?"

I furrowed my brow. "This is the time you pick to ask about that?" My eyes flickered toward him, then back to the boats, but I answered. "Yeah, I'm pretty sure. She'd been with Dad since high school. He couldn't have kept something like this from her."

I watched the men wander the dock. They were clearly waiting for someone or something. I just hoped it was Nefasto.

"Do you think that's why she left?" Mitch asked.

"I don't know. Maybe. But if it was about Dad's secret life, why not divorce him? Why not take us with her? She left us Mitch. She took off. Whatever her reasons, it doesn't change the fact that she gave us up and didn't look back."

Mitch opened his mouth to respond, but the men were starting to move. The engine of one of the boats roared to life. "Darn it." His eyebrows sank into a deep-V. "What if the money transfer was digital? An online transaction? What if Nefasto doesn't show? Why didn't we think of—"

"Wait," I cut him off, pointing to a set of headlights sweeping through the dark boneyard of industrial equipment. "Look."

A dark blue '56 Chevrolet Bel Air pulled up. Another Yank tank, only this one was pristine and perfectly restored.

The classic car rolled to a stop fifty yards away from the wooden dock. My chin sank against my forearm with relief. Nefasto slowly got out and approached the now semicircle of Scandinavian men.

"This is good," I said. "He came alone, which means he should leave alone." I pulled my gun from the back of my pants and did a quick press check to make sure a round was in the chamber.

"Let's just stick to the plan," Andy said, putting a hand on my wrist. "Don't start shooting people yet."

I held back a smile. "Yes, sir."

We both looked in unison as a large blond man emerged from the shadows. His long flowing hair seemed to contrast the expensive suit he wore. After approaching Nefasto, he extended a metal briefcase. "Delivery payment, part two of two. Yes?"

"Yes," Nefasto nodded.

As he held out his hand to grab the case, the Scandinavian man pulled it back. "I was told we'd be given a demonstration of the new models."

"Don't you watch the news?"

"Yes. The embassy. Impressive, but that was the old model. I'd like to see the new ones for myself. In person."

Nefasto nodded, then motioned to one of the armed Cuban men, who pulled a missile out of one of the cases.

"See those barges?" Nefasto said, pointing out to the water.

Two hundred yards from the dock, two large barges

stacked with wooden containers bobbed in the water.

"I see them."

Nefasto motioned once more to the Cuban man who shouldered the slender tube-like missile effortlessly. He triggered it and–*whoosh*–it screamed off into the air, cleared the distance in a second and both barges instantly imploded. They completely folded on themselves, yanked together with a sonic boom that sucked everything in before rubber-banding back and sending a circular ten-foot-high wake out in every direction. As the water calmed, the target was so disintegrated, there was barely any debris left in the water.

"Now you see it, now you don't," Nefasto said. "That is the genius of Castillo. He is the Da Vinci of our time. If you were to buy the same type of missile from anyone else, you would need a mounted platform to launch it. Any other weapon capable of the same penetration and mechanical stress would be ten times as large, twenty times as heavy. No one builds weapons smaller, more easy to transport, or capable of more destruction than Castillo."

"You may be right." The Scandinavian nodded, clearly impressed.

"Soon, you will be able to level an entire city with weapons you can fit in the trunk of your car," Nefasto said with a smile that quickly evaporated. "Now...the money, please."

The Scandinavian handed Nefasto the briefcase, then turned to his men. "Keep loading," he shouted.

Up on the metal container I lay frozen in shock. The missile test had sent a fresh wave of terror down my spine. I'd seen videos of the embassy explosion, but witnessing it in person shook my confidence. I watched as men patrolled the area. Nefasto's guys covered the street, the Scandinavians had the dock. Three or four paced in alternating patterns past Nefasto's car. I tried to memorize their paths, but there were too many.

I pulled Mitch back further out of sight. "Give me your phone." He hesitated, but I snatched it from his hand. "This is the app? Is it all set up?"

"Yeah, but I thought I was going to plant—"

"Forget it. It's too risky. Just let me do my thing. Both of you wait here. I'll be back—"

"You can't do this all yourself," Mitch cut in. "When are you going to trust me?"

"It's not a matter of trust."

"He's right," Andy said. "There are too many moving parts for one person."

I set my jaw, considering it. "Okay. We split things in half. I'll plant the phone and create the distraction. You and Mitch are in charge of securing the boat."

"Great," Mitch said. "How do we do that?"

"Use my distraction."

"Right. And what does that mean?"

Before I could answer, one of the Scandinavian men's voices boomed. "Let's go!"

Andy turned quickly to Mitch. "We will figure it

out."

Mitch let out a shaky breath. "Perfect."

"You good?" I asked Mitch.

His eyes swept the dock, pulling all the pieces together. "Yeah, go do your thing. Just...don't die."

"Don't die. Got it." I shimmied toward the edge of the container, my gut tight with worry.

Andy caught my arm and pulled himself closer. "They see you, they kill you."

"I've trained for this. It's what I'm good at."

He held my gaze, but another boat fired up its engine and he loosened his grip.

"Be careful," he whispered.

I nodded and slunk off the container, heading toward Nefasto's car. Moving fast, but with practiced tactical precision, I stayed low, hidden in shadows and along narrow sightlines, always out of view.

One of Castillo's men lingered near the vehicle, but faced away toward the dock. I kept crouched and silent as I slid behind Nefasto's car, using the side mirror to make sure I wasn't noticed, then opened the door with quiet ease. Listening for the sound of footsteps, I leaned forward and slipped the phone under the driver's seat. Once it was in place, I partially shut the door and then leaned on it to get the lock to catch with a gentle snap.

Without warning, the man beside the car turned, lighting a cigarette. I ducked down, unsure if he saw me or heard the door latch. His feet shuffled in my direction, and I raised my gun, ready to fire, but he slowly turned back away. I exhaled quietly, then spun and slid back into the shadows.

On the opposite side of the dock, I glimpsed Mitch and Andy for the briefest second making their way around several giant containers. I needed to make my move. Thinking quickly, I headed along a covered straightaway, but as I rounded the side of a rust-colored unit, I abruptly slid to a halt. There, twenty yards straight ahead, was another gunman. A short Cuban with a gun dangling from his hand.

I froze and pressed against the container. The cold metal shocked my skin as my eyes darted from side to side, searching for a way out. There was another container fifty feet to my left, but if I ran, the short man would surely spot me. My eyes ticked right, but there was only wide-open, brightly lit space and a large red crane.

I spun and looked behind me. A small recess where a second container butted up against this one cast a dark shadow, but was it dark enough to provided complete cover? I heard the man heading toward me. It was my only option.

I lurched for the recess, pressing as flat as I could. Doing a quick test, I held out my hand in front of my face. It was dark, but I could still see the outline of my fingers. I briefly considered running back, but the point became moot as the man stepped into view. He cocked his pistol and scanned the area.

I held my breath, cementing my feet to the ground, afraid to even blink.

The man turned directly toward me and squinted, trying to peer through the darkness. As he raised his gun and pointed it toward the shadows, I slowly reached for mine.

My chest grew tight.

I stared down at the man's feet, gauging his next move. He pressed onto the balls of his feet, but something stopped him—a noise or a voice in the distance. He turned. My opportunity to take him down. Moving on instinct, I shot forward, twisting the gun from his hand and hooked his neck in the crook of my arm, wrapping him in a chokehold. He clawed at my wrist, but I secured my grip with my other hand and monkey-climbed onto his back so he couldn't trip up my feet. In less than a minute the man seized up and let out a choking sound.

When he went slack, I dragged his unconscious body into the shadows, then picked up his pistol, shucked the clip to check for rounds, and racked the chamber.

Whatever I was going to do, I had to do it fast. My mind played out Mitch and Andy's part of the plan. Once we took one of the boats, the other two were sure to follow. The area was teeming with men, and the final boat was loaded. If I could find a way to take out the other vessels along with the buyers, maybe use one of the explosives...

The massive red crane twenty yards to the right

caught my eye. Attached to the end of its arm was a container box, ready to be moved. I didn't have time to think of an alternative. I exhaled, taking a moment to calm my heart before sprinting forward across the well-lit open space.

As I climbed into the glass encasement, I glanced behind me. Nobody had spotted me...yet. I sat in the control seat, but began to panic in my search for the keys. They weren't under the seat or in the side panel of the door. I started considering other methods, but found them hanging from the ignition. Apparently, no one was worried about a random American girl hijacking an industrial crane at a Cuban port.

Once I familiarized myself with the controls, essentially a joystick on each armrest, one for side-to-side movement and the other for raising and lowing the crane arm, I scanned the dock for any sign of Mitch or Andy. The Scandinavians still occupied the boats, and the long-haired one was shaking hands with Nefasto, signaling completion of the deal.

It was now or never.

As the head buyer moved toward the boats to leave, everyone, including Nefasto, paused at the odd mechanical sound that floated through the air, a mix of gears turning and metal scraping as I attempted to move the metal container. The men in the boats, finally looked up and located the source of the noise. I positioned the giant metal shipping container directly over the dock and right above their heads.

Before they could run I pushed the release button—*click.* The container fell, and the men scattered as the huge metal box dropped. It fell fifty feet in the air, completely destroying two of the boats and nearly eviscerating most of the wooden dock. Shards of wood and cement sprayed into the air like deadly confetti.

Nefasto staggered backward and stared at the aftermath. His face went red as he turned and saw that it was me who manned the crane.

"Kill her!" he screamed.

Nefasto's men charged toward me, and my heart knocked wildly in my chest, but I waited. I needed this vantage point to see if Andy and Mitch could secure the other boat.

"Come on," I whispered to myself, tapping my fingers on the joystick.

As if they'd heard me, the two of them slipped unnoticed behind the Scandinavians at the dock, and I watched the other two boats sink to the bottom of the port.

With little time to escape, and men surrounding the crane, I saw only one way out. It wasn't my best option, but it was all I had. I moved the crane arm back over the water, then slipped out the door of the glass cab and climbed onto the metal roof.

Someone fired four successive shots near the boats. The sound stopped me where I was, and I caught Andy out of the corner of my eye taking down the buyers who remained on the dock.

As they writhed in pain, he hopped in their remaining boat, and started it up. He throttled forward, and I leapt onto the diagonal arm of the crane, climbing as fast as I could toward the top.

As Nefasto and his men unloaded, a fusillade of bullets ricocheted off the metal below my feet. I tried not to think of how exposed I was. Fear coaxed me onward, though my hands slipped against the steel frame of the arm, and my feet moved faster than my confidence. One misstep and I would fall.

Below, Andy gunned the boat in my direction. My way out.

A hail of lead chased me to the top of the arm, fifty feet in the air, but trapped me at the very end with no more room to run. Nefasto climbed onto the crane body and aimed his gun at me. Just before it went off, I jumped.

No hesitation, no looking back. My stomach lifted into my throat and I held my breath as I tensed for impact. I kept my body straight as I plummeted into the cool water, feet first, and it hit me like a slap. Pain shot from my heels to my spine and bubbles rose around me in a dizzying spiral before I swam up for air.

"You okay?" Mitch shouted as I surfaced. I gave a thumbs up, though I wasn't entirely sure, and Andy slowed down just enough for Mitch to throw over a rope. I reached for it, snagging it with one hand, but Nefasto and his men raked the side of the boat with bullets. Andy cried out and slapped a hand to his deltoid muscle. Blood seeped through his fingers as he pushed the engine to its max.

My heart gave a lurch as I floated behind them, knowing what was about to happen. The rope went taut, and whipped me out of the way of a second wave of bullets that buried harmlessly into the sea.

"Get us out of here," I yelled, unable to take cover in the open water.

Andy steered for a bend in the coast, and jammed the throttle forward, dragging me away. The tension yanked me so hard I caught air, and my chest nearly burst from the sheer terror of being flung behind a moving speedboat. I let out an involuntary scream before landing back into the ocean with an excruciating smack. The wake broke around my body and I gasped and choked on the spray, which felt like being waterboarded. As the boat dragged me along the surface of the water I tried to hold my breath, gritting my teeth against the sting of the water and dreading the inevitable pain to come. Still, I kept a tight grip on the rope. Within seconds, the sound of gunfire faded behind me, and Andy zoomed around the next bend.

Gone like smoke.

CHAPTER TWENTY-ONE

THE SUN HAD BROKEN the surface of the horizon. Its light splintered through the clouds and stained them with color. As soon as we were out of range, Mitch pulled me in. I let him do the work, allowing my beaten body to float like a doll through the lapping water as I coughed out the liquid in my lungs and tried to breathe.

Andy helped him hoist me onto the floor of the boat, and I closed my eyes, as we sped away. The early morning air whipped at my wet clothes, chilling me into a shiver, but I didn't care. I was alive. We all were. For now.

After a long, bumpy ride that shook every inch of my sore body, Andy navigated the boat into a lush embankment overgrown with mangrove trees. The hull of the go-fast scraped against the shallow bottom of the shore, but he managed to hide it behind a dense collection of tree roots.

In a rush, he killed the engine and knelt at my side. His hands swept over my arms and legs, his eyes searching for injuries. "Are you hurt?"

Mitch stood behind him, his face tight with worry.

I sat up with a groan. The torque from the boat had tossed my vertebrae around like dice, but I refused to acknowledge the pain. The Marines had taught me to ignore it. To push past superficial injuries and complete the mission. "No, I'm okay."

"Can you stand?" Andy asked, helping me up.

I nodded, but kept hold of his strong shoulders.

"Did you plant the phone?" Mitch's voice was laced with doubt. "If so, we need to get to a computer."

"It's in there," I answered.

"I know a place that's open twenty-four hours." Andy held my waist with firm hands. "If you think you can make it. It's close."

I ignored the shooting pain in my right hip and pulled away, standing on my own. "I'm fine," I said, disregarding my body's cry for rest. "Let's go."

The three of us climbed over the side of the boat, wetting our legs to the knees as we made for land. It only took several minutes of speed walking behind Andy before "close" felt like an eternity. Every time I turned a corner, I tensed for an ambush. The people wandering the streets paid no attention to our wet legs and rushing feet. To them, it was just another day. But I eyed each one suspiciously, imagining they were all spies for Castillo.

Finally, Andy opened the door to an Internet café with only a few exhausted looking patrons. We sat in the back, grouping our chairs around a single computer screen. I turned to check the front door, in case we were followed, and winced involuntarily at the sharp jolt in my lower back.

"You okay?" Andy asked, watching me.

"Fine." I looked up, catching sight of his bleeding shoulder. I'd completely forgotten he'd been shot. "Andy, your—"

"It's nothing," he answered. He lifted his sleeve to reveal the track of the bullet. "Grazed the skin."

I sighed in quiet relief as Mitch used the hem of his shirt to wipe down the computer screen. It was filthy. Coffee stains, finger prints and a thick, unrecognizable film blurred the pixels. But it was all we had. I hoped it would work.

"Okay, got it," Mitch said after navigating to the correct site and logging in.

On screen in front of us, the tracking app showed a blinking blue dot over a Google-type satellite map, signifying the location of Mitch's phone. He zoomed in on what had to be Castillo's latest safe house. It was an enormous mansion, surrounded by a giant cement wall.

"Check it out." Mitch slid his chair over and let me in to click and zoom around the property.

After a few minutes I leaned back and rubbed my face. "I dunno." I zoomed in again, clicking different parts of the screen. "Every angle I come at it from feels like a suicide mission. What good is knowing where Castillo is, if we can't get to him?"

Mitch had a desperate look in his eyes, and I knew exactly how he felt. We were so close.

"We just have to think outside the box," he said.

"You're the brains here. Any ideas?"

Mitch took a few seconds to think. "Have you ever heard of Marcel Proust?"

"Oh, yeah," I teased. "He's a good friend of mine."

"I don't get it," Andy said. "Who is he?"

Mitch laughed. "He was a French Essayist."

"Oh, *that* Marcel Proust," I said with a smirk.

"He said, 'The real magic of discovery lies not in seeking new landscapes but in having new eyes.' The point being, we have to look at this differently and find a more creative route."

"And..." I gestured for him to elaborate, "how exactly do we do that?"

"Walk me through it. What are their defenses?"

I pointed at the computer screen. "Aside from the gigantic wall..."

"We know he'll have armed men, inside and out," Andy pointed out.

"Any decent close proximity protection team would have at least ten men for an environment that size," I continued. "If I had to guess, I'd say six outside, four inside. But that's not counting the security-trained drivers for the Escalades."

"Okay," Mitch said, pursing his lips. "It's clear we're not getting in...we'll just have to get him to come out. Grab him on the move."

"We tried that before," Andy mentioned. "It backfired."

"Exactly," I added. "Once he gets in one of those Escalades, he's inside a rolling panic room."

"Hang on. Not necessarily. Same logic applies to the SUVs. If we can't get in, we get him to come out."

I shook my head. "Would never happen. Trust me, I've been inside one of those armored vehicles. Even with the right tools it would take hours to get someone out."

Mitch rubbed his temples and stretched his neck downward. He stared hard at the Google map and the area surrounding the house, then tapped a section of the screen. "What's all this? These dark lines?" he asked.

"Canal system," Andy answered. He slid his finger across the map. "These canals run all through Havana and dump out into the ocean."

Mitch pounded the table in excitement and everyone in the place turned. He held up an apologetic hand, and they all went back to what they were doing.

"That's it," Mitch whispered. "That's how we do it. We use the canals."

"Okay," I said. "Talk slow and tell us what you're thinking."

But Mitch was already all up in his head. "We're going

to need some equipment." His gaze turned to the front glass doors of the Internet café where a large delivery truck sat parked alongside the curb. "And...I can't believe I'm actually suggesting this, but I think you're going to need to steal that truck."

THE THREE OF us stood inside Andy's open storage unit.

"I've got the guns packed up, but where are the paintballs?" Mitch asked.

"These?" I tossed over a package of bright yellow orbs sitting in front of me on a shelf, and Mitch shoved them in one of the several packed duffle bags at his feet before heading for the back of the truck.

"Is that it?" Andy asked, stepping close to me. "We shouldn't be here. Word will have spread. Castillo will have a large bounty out. I'm sure people are looking for us."

"I know."

He brushed his hand against my cheek and I leaned in without thought, pressing my lips to his. "Sorry..." I said, instantly pulling back, unsure about it. "I—"

"Don't be." Andy moved in closer, and kissed me again. His fingers slipped into my hair and my heart beat harder.

"All loaded up," Mitch said. He paused and saw us

inches apart, then pretended to be studying the painted mural on the unit next to us. Ten feet high bulbous letters spelled out: "Revolución" with a giant cartoon fist behind it. "Right, so...uh...you guys probably...I'm gonna wait in the truck."

I let out a sigh, preparing myself for what lay ahead. No matter how many down-in-the-dirt, fight-for-your-life experiences I'd had, nothing terrified me like this. Losing my family would break me.

I kept it together, burying my fear and ignoring the tight knot of panic in my gut. My only comforting thought was that I knew I had it in me. I'd do what needed to be done. Whatever it took.

"Ready for this?" I asked.

Andy laced his fingers through mine. "I guess we'll see."

CHAPTER TWENTY-TWO

I KEPT HIDDEN, BELLY-DOWN behind a cluster of brush, and surveyed the mansion through a pair of binoculars. Behind me, Mitch and Andy dug a hole, a big one. Dirt flew over their shoulders, pattering the ground like heavy rain.

I sat up and Mitch paused to wipe his brow. "Any sign of him?"

"No," I answered. "But he's in there. A full security team is in place."

The house was enormous. In the backyard an Olympic-sized infinity pool, finished with indigo-mirrored glass tile, created the illusion of water spilling into nowhere. Nine-foot-high concrete walls circled the compound, protecting the occupants from prying eyes and would-be intruders. Inside them, the armed men guarding the house looked hardened and efficient. They flaunted a distinct air of menace as they wandered the grounds, alert for threats.

Outside the walls, I spotted motion detectors that provided an early warning system. Infrared beams criss-crossed the expanse, ensuring nothing could penetrate undetected. Luckily, Andy had led us up a back road into one of the hills behind the home, so the three of us weren't visible from this vantage point.

"Almost there," Andy said, nodding at the ground. "Keep going."

Mitch went back to digging and launched more dirt over his head. After a few more rounds, they struck metal. I crawled to the edge and watched Andy brush the loose soil away to reveal four pipes.

"You sure this will work?" I asked, leaning over the hole.

Mitch looked up. "Relax, it's basic science. An eighth grader could do it."

"Which is which?" I motioned to the pipes.

Andy pointed to one. "This is the natural gas line. We'll feed that into this water line, which feeds the sprinkler system," he said, pointing to the other.

I turned to Mitch. "Okay, have at it, Einstein."

"I prefer Niels Bohr."

"Who's that?" I asked without thinking.

"He developed the Bohr model of the atom," Mitch answered. "He won the Nobel Prize in Physics in 1922."

I handed him the toolbox. "If you can make this happen, I'll call you whatever you want." I watched as Mitch began to work on the two small pipes. "I'm just glad that high IQ is on my side, not theirs."

He nodded, the recognition of his value putting a small smile on his face.

"Okay." He tightened something with a wrench and stepped out of the hole. "It's go time."

Andy hopped out next and jogged to the delivery truck, which was camouflaged with carefully placed tree branches. He bounced onto the hood, readied his paintball gun and gave us both a thumbs up.

I nodded. This was it. One shot. If I missed my mark, those precious seconds could blow our cover. I shook my right hand, loosening up my fingers, racked my gun, then lay down in front of a fallen tree, using the log to steady my aim.

One shot. With a slow exhale, I held my breath and fired. The bullet hit a sprinkler head thirty yards away, just as I'd hoped. The spark immediately ignited the natural gas being pumped from the pipes Mitch had rerouted. The resulting explosion from the spark raced through the pipe system, across the entire yard and caused every sprinkler on the grounds to catch fire. And with a rapid series of concussive booms, the entire lawn exploded with 12-foot-high geysers of flame.

I grinned, eyes wide. "I'll be damned. It worked."

From here, I had a perfect view of the mansion. The guards outside went crazy, running around confused as they tried to put out the fires. Within seconds, the front door burst open. The guards, led by Nefasto, formed a semicircle around Castillo, creating a human shield. They escorted him to one of the four Escalades and put him inside.

Up on the truck, Andy immediately took aim and fired his rifle.

"You sure you got this?" I called, jaunting toward him. "I was trained by one of the best marksmen—"

A single paintball struck one of the rims, and he smirked at me. "Done."

The lone, yellow dot now marked the SUV Castillo was in. I took a moment to smile at Andy as he climbed down.

"Okay, not bad," I conceded as all three of us hopped inside the truck.

I threw the vehicle into drive, and Mitch turned to me. "This is it, you know that, right? We don't get Castillo now, we'll never get another chance...and Dad's dead for sure."

My eyes stayed focused on the Escalade. "We'll get him."

"Put in your bits," Andy said tossing us both plastic molded mouth guards. "This is going to hurt."

Castillo and his convoy of Escalades whooshed along the only stretch of highway that led away from the mansion. I lost sight of them as I navigated down the backroad of our hill and onto a residential street. But we'd already mapped it out. There were no turnoffs, and we knew exactly where to cut them off. I jammed my foot down on the accelerator, heading to the first intersection that would cross their path. We couldn't miss this opportunity. The truck teetered around quiet street corners with thick palm trees and luxurious houses. I spun the wheel, ignoring Mitch's terrified face and his white-knuckled grip.

As we approached a three-way stop, I could see their convoy approaching. They'd changed positions several times, but I knew where to look. The line of vehicles had slowed their speed to a more reasonable forty miles per hour. Whoever was coordinating their movements must have figured the danger was behind them.

I slowed as well, matching their pace and trying to time things just right. They'd assume I would yield, but that wasn't the plan. As the Escalade with the yellow rim rolled through the intersection, I exploded past the stop sign slamming into the marked vehicle's side.

The collision was so sudden and violent, I instantly lost control. My head hit the wheel with a hard smack, and the last thing I glimpsed was the Escalade flipping onto its side and skidding twenty feet before careening into the canal.

I WOKE IN a daze to Andy shaking my shoulder. Cold water had seeped in through the doors soaking my feet, and it took me a moment to realize I'd lost consciousness and our truck had followed the Escalade into the canal. Thankfully, that was the plan.

"Get your gear on," I shouted as the truck sank deeper.

Andy and I scrambled to secure our tanks, but Mitch sat in shock, rushing water rising past his waist.

"Mitch!" I yelled. My voice seemed to jar him from his stupor, and he shouldered his air tank.

When the water reached my chin, I dove under. The cool, murky liquid pressed in around me, muting and distorting all sound. Andy followed soon after and began kicking at the windshield. I hoisted my legs to help, and a moment later, the three of us swam out, fully equipped with scuba gear. Fifteen feet down, at the bottom of the algae-coated canal, I spotted the Escalade's headlights illuminating the ground around it. Even the dome light in the vehicle was lit as I headed toward it.

As Andy and Mitch swam up, I spotted Castillo through the side window. He slowly stirred as water poured in all around him. I nodded to Mitch and winked through my mask. The SUV might be bullet proof, but it wasn't waterproof. And the collision had only exacerbated the condition. As I pressed against the glass to get a closer look, I saw the water flow escalate by the second; it gushed inside. Bottom line was, we no longer needed to get into the rolling fortress, this would force Castillo out.

I unsheathed a knife and knocked on the window with the butt of it. The driver sat unconscious, but Castillo's eyes were wide open, terrified and alert. He undid his seatbelt and sloshed around the vehicle. The water was already up to his chest as I knocked again. Castillo finally spotted us and his face filled with anger. As he pressed close to the window, Mitch held up a spare tank and waved him out.

Inside, Castillo furiously grabbed a loose semi-automatic gun and aimed it at me, but then he dropped the gun, no doubt remembering the glass was bullet proof on his side, too. As I shook my head and waved him out, the water rose to his neck. Out of options, he reluctantly pressed the emergency latch, which unhooked the entire door.

The Escalade opened up and expelled Castillo, a breech birth into the dark, cold water. He tried to swim away, but I grabbed him and put a knife to his neck, allowing Andy to jam a regulator into his mouth.

My chest throbbed with urgency and anticipation. *We had him. We did it.*

With a wave of satisfaction, I dragged Castillo to one of Andy's anchored Dive Propulsion Vehicles, throttled it forward and the four of us sped away from the Escalade's lights into the inky darkness.

CHAPTER TWENTY-THREE

MOONLIGHT PRESSED AGAINST the tangled branches of mangrove trees encircling our stolen boat. A soaking-wet Castillo sat near the back, seething, not the least bit repentant for his transgressions. His hands and feet were bound, and he glared at me as I searched the boat for things I could use. Luckily, we'd caught the Scandinavians by surprise, and I lifted a loose cell phone and a handgun from one of the boat's side compartments.

Castillo let out a laugh and shook his head. "I bet you think you've got this all under control—"

"Shut up, no one's interested in what you have to say," I snapped.

"No? You're not wondering how Daddy's doing? Is he dead? Alive? Did I torture him—"

I lunged for him, ignoring the stab of pain that radiated from my hip up my spine, and smashed the butt of my new gun into his mouth, splitting his lip. "If he's dead, you're dead."

Castillo spit blood. "You are so easy to manipulate, Chica. You are, what do the Americans call it? A hothead."

"You are, what do I call it? A douche bag."

Castillo laughed, blood dripping from his chin. "Sí, sí, sí. So, what now? I assume the plan is to make a trade. Me for your father, correct?"

"That's right," Mitch answered from across the boat, his voice stern and even.

Castillo glanced at Andy, then turned to me again. "And I suppose you think that will be it. You think that's where this ends?"

"Pretty much." My grip tightened on the gun in my hand as I resisted the urge to shoot him. A bullet to the shin wouldn't be fatal. I could do it.

"I'm afraid not." Castillo shook his head. "See, you've made this personal, and I am a prideful man...to a fault." His eyes flickered toward Andy again. "Your friend can tell you all about that, though."

Andy stood up. "Tara, don't—"

I held up a hand, stopping him from moving closer. It was always best to let the captor talk in case they gave something away. "Meaning?" I prompted.

"Well, you can't kill me if you want to keep Daddy alive. And once I'm returned, once I'm free again..." Castillo answered. "I will never let this drop. Never. And at some point, I will find you again."

"Maybe you could just send flowers."

As I walked away, Castillo's words became more desperate. He turned to Mitch. "You are the smart one, boy, look at me and tell me I'm lying."

Mitch turned to Castillo, and I could tell he was trying to play it cool, but the man's eyes were like two chips of stone and Mitch's shoulders tensed. "Just do us all a favor and sit there quietly," he murmured.

"I will send men for all of you. Maybe not right away. But some day. Maybe when you're a little older. I may prolong it so you have to constantly look over your shoulders. So that you will be afraid to make friends or take lovers knowing that anyone close to you would be in danger as well. Think about it. I will ruin your lives for years and years before I finally choose to end them."

I knew how far his reach extended. If we did pull off this trade, what he said was most likely true, and the threat sank deep into my bones.

Andy pushed past me and shoved Castillo back. "Enough talking. Callate la boca."

"And *you*," Castillo continued. "You'll be easy. I already know where your family is. Last time I swatted you away like a pesky gnat. This time, I will keep you close, really make you suffer. You will have no life worth living before I take it from you."

Andy's jaw clenched, but his lips stayed pressed shut. Blood was beginning to seep through the wet sleeve of his shirt from the bullet graze.

My gut twisted with guilt, but I pulled out the Scandinavian's phone. There was no going back now. "Let's get this over with." I pointed my gun at Castillo's knee. "Nefasto's number or I shoot you in the leg. And don't tempt me, because I really, really want to do it."

He kept his face void of emotion, but complied, telling me the number.

"Hello," Nefasto's familiar voice piped out of the cell phone pressed to my ear.

"Nefasto," I said. "You know who this is."

"Yes—"

"Don't talk, listen. You have two hours to take possession of my father. Keep your phone nearby. I'll call you with details for the exchange."

"Wait—"

I hung up without letting him respond, and slapped duct tape over Castillo's mouth, not wanting to hear his voice anymore. As I turned away from him, Mitch motioned me to the front of the boat, out of earshot.

"He isn't kidding," Andy whispered. "Those things he said."

"Does he know you?" Mitch asked, trying to fill in the missing pieces.

"It's a long story," I answered.

Mitch's face tightened, but he let it drop. "He's right, though. We give Castillo back, and how long before he shows up at our doorstep? How long until he kills us, kills Dad, or someone else we care about?"

"And it won't stop with us," Andy added. "How many future deaths around the world will he be responsible for? How many terrorists will he supply, how many wars will Castillo contribute to? We can't give him back."

"You heard Nefasto's sales pitch," Mitch continued. "With the arsenal Castillo's developing, they'll be able to level a city with weapons you could fit in a car trunk." He shook his head and looked up at me. "I should be happy that we got him, but exchanging him for Dad doesn't feel right. Dad wouldn't want this. He knows how dangerous Castillo is. He thought it was important enough to risk his life to get this guy."

I stared past Mitch and into the hateful eyes behind him. "What are you saying?"

"I'm saying we have to consider leaving, right now with Castillo. Get him into custody where he can't hurt anyone anymore."

Mitch's plan clicked, and I flinched with shock. "And leave Dad?"

"Castillo's the head of the snake. Cut the head and the body dies. I don't *want* to leave him, but how many lives do we save if we bring Castillo in? What would Dad want us to do?"

I rubbed my face with both hands. Mitch was right. But screw logic. I wanted my dad back. "No," I said. "I don't care. I'm not leaving Dad." I'd come too far to give up on him. It couldn't end like this. Not after everything we'd been through.

"Tara..."

I looked up, truly vulnerable in front of Mitch for the first time. Desperation drummed in my chest and the full body ache I'd been pushing away drove deeper into my bones. "Please, just think. There's gotta be one more plan in that big brain."

Andy turned to Mitch. "Is there some way for you to go home with Castillo *and* your father?"

Mitch took a seat and closed his eyes.

I sat down beside him, using every fiber of my being to will him into an answer.

Mitch's eyes finally snapped open. "I think I have something."

"What?" I insisted. "Tell me."

"It would be insanely dangerous, but..."

My fingertips dug into my bruised, bare thighs. "But what?"

"It's within the faint realm of possibility."

I STOOD WITH Andy inside his storage unit as Mitch loaded additional gear into yet another stolen truck, this time with Castillo tied up in the back. My head ticked back and forth as I scanned the alley. I didn't like being here, but so far no one had showed and there'd been nothing to suggest anyone had been here. Maybe Jorge never got the chance to tell Nefasto about Andy, but I couldn't ignore the risk.

"This plan of his is insane, you know that." Andy stared at me, eyebrows arched, as I finished bandaging his wounded arm.

"Completely," I answered.

He dragged a hand through his tousled dark hair and sighed. "I mean there is dangerous and then there is this plan."

My gaze drifted toward Mitch as he sorted all the gear. It was divided by type of excursion: diving tours, base jumping tours, kayak & snorkel adventures, zip-line tours, etc. His plan called for a little bit of each. He rifled through specific piles, jammed what he needed into large duffle bags and lifted them over his shoulder with a grunt.

"Believe me...I know." I smiled half-heartedly and reached for Andy's hand. "But it's all we've got."

Mitch walked past us, struggling to carry the heavy equipment. "No really, you guys just take it easy. Good ol' Mitch will finish loading up all the gear. Just keep staring into each others' eyes."

I laughed as Andy leaned in to kiss me, but Mitch returned in seconds, exhaling sarcastically. "Okay two things...one, I'm about to vomit. Two, I'm done loading the van."

"I guess we should go, then." I let Andy's fingers slip from mine.

We all hopped into the van, and I yanked out the Scandinavian's cell phone to call Nefasto.

As he answered, I gripped the phone hard. "Listen carefully. I'm going to give you instructions and then hang up, so you'd better be writing this down."

"I'm listening..."

CHAPTER TWENTY-FOUR

THE EARLY MORNING SUN, while not yet visible above Avila Mountain, still brightened the sky. It slowly worked its way up, breaching a wide wall of clouds. Iridescent reds and pinks bled into each other like watercolors as a thick, swirling wind swept across the mountaintop.

At a large metal platform near the summit, Mitch and I waited beside one of the two available cable cars. They were empty, as was the rest of the gondola lift. According to Andy, it wouldn't open for tourists for another two hours.

Castillo sat at my feet, still bound and looking smug as I stretched forward and peered through binoculars. The ground below resembled a bisectional ant farm. All around the base of the mountain, twenty different river outlets cut through the ground. The water spider-webbed across the landmass and eventually headed to the ocean.

I focused in on a specific section where Andy waited with our stolen boat, my chest tightening with worry. I'd tried to push my feelings for him away in the beginning, but there was no denying them now. The heart was a stubborn thing. If something happened to him, it was going to hurt. The vulnerability sat like a rock in my stomach. It was very possible at least one of us wouldn't make it out of this alive.

My phone rang. I snapped to attention and answered it. The strong wind died and the whole world seemed to wait.

"I have your father," Nefasto's voice said through the phone.

My stomach unclenched with relief.

"Let me see," I replied and turned the binoculars to the adjacent cable car platform at the base of the mountain. I found Nefasto, who was flanked by five armed thugs. Behind them was a man, hands bound, with a cloth sack over his head.

"Here he is," Nefasto announced.

I pulled the phone away, turned to Mitch. "I think I see Dad."

I put the phone back up and focused my binoculars. Down below, Nefasto pushed the bound man into view and yanked off the hood. *It was him.* He was weak, soaked with sweat and blood, and his face was severely swollen. He stumbled and had to be held up by two of Nefasto's men. I stared, flush with emotion. Tears brimmed in my eyes, spilling onto my cheeks. He was alive. My heart shed its hard shell, and reached for him.

"Now Castillo," Nefasto's voice returned.

I nodded to Mitch. "Show him."

Mitch yanked Castillo to his feet and pushed him forward, closer to the edge of the platform, holding him by the shoulders.

"I see him," Nefasto confirmed. "Now what?"

I paused. "Now the exchange. We control the cars. They will go at the exact same time, at my command. Understand?"

"Agreed. But if I see Castillo's car so much as pause, your father is dead."

Nefasto put the cloth hood back over Dad's head and shoved him into the cable car. As he shut the door, all of the armed men aimed their guns.

"Okay," I said to Mitch. "Let's do this."

He headed to the control box, a small open-air office near the back of the platform that housed the only set of gondola controls, leaving me with Castillo. The tape over his mouth had partially come loose. I peeled it off slowly and painfully, just to see him wince.

"Come on," I said, shoving him toward the cable car. I threw open the door and positioned him in front of it.

Castillo looked over his shoulder at me and smiled. "We will meet again, my friend."

I muted the phone. "Sooner than you think, shitface."

As a confused look fell over Castillo, I put a foot on

his butt and kicked him into the cable car. He flew to the far end, slammed against the metal wall and slumped down to the ground. I gave him a hard wink and slammed the door shut.

I nodded to Mitch, and unmuted the phone. "Nefasto. We're ready. Cars moving in 3... 2...1..."

After I gave the hand signal to Mitch, he set the gondola in motion.

With a loud thunk, the two cable cars at either end moved at the same time. As they headed toward each other, I hung up the phone.

Mitch ran back carrying one of the duffels filled with gear, and the two of us took up positions next to the thick metal cables supporting the cars.

"Now?" I asked.

Mitch watched the cars with narrowed eyes, as if performing calculations in his head on the fly. Down below, all of the armed men kept aim on Dad's car as it sped away.

"Not yet," Mitch said. "About thirty more seconds."

"There is a really good chance this ends badly." I couldn't look away from my little brother, and secretly hoped he'd chicken out. "If you wanna bail, I can make the jump."

"No way." Mitch shook his head and slipped on a small backpack. He handed a similar one to me. "Let's be honest, there's no way you'll pull this off without me."

"True." I turned back toward the cable cars, hoping

he hadn't seen the fear in my eyes. As much as I wished he'd stay back, I knew he was right. I needed him. "I meant what I said before. I'm glad you're here." My stomach tensed as I imagined him plummeting toward the ground and falling to his death.

Mitch glanced at me and smiled. "Dad once told me... as sure as people live, they die. But as long as they do both with purpose, there's never much to regret."

"I like that," I said, swallowing down my nerves. "Let's hope we live."

"Ready?" Mitch asked as the cable cars started to distance themselves from the platforms. "Now!"

With this, we sprang into action, attaching modified zip-line devices to the thick metal cable overhead and without another word, leapt outward. I braced myself for the pain of the harness against my already sore upper body. The zip-line hooks caught snuggly and carried us forward. Mitch let out a small gasp as the earth below our feet fell away. My heart raced with the familiar thrill of a mission.

This was going to work. We were almost there.

As we zipped down the wire, the ground, now thousands of feet below, blurred deliriously. Distant gun fire began to pop in erratic succession, but we were out of range, and I knew Dad would be smart enough to take cover. I glanced back at Mitch who had a grimace plastered on his face. I had to admit, I was impressed. During my first high altitude skydive I had to be forcibly thrown out of the plane. Mitch hadn't even hesitated. The kid had guts.

As I turned back, we were nearly on Castillo's cable car. At ten feet away, I pulled the gun from my waistband, steading myself with my other hand. At five feet away, I shot the glass out of the back door, just before slamming into the car. On impact, I let out a pain-induced groan, but managed to grip the doorframe and twist inside.

Mitch arrived moments later. I leaned out to secure him then yanked him into the cable car. We both turned to each other and let out equally heavy sighs, stunned that this first part even worked.

"Are you two insane?" Castillo's voice came from behind.

I lunged for him, but Mitch stopped me. "Please...let me."

He pulled back his fist and dropped Castillo with a hard right. The man fell to the floor, unconscious.

"What the..." I whispered, in shock.

Mitch turned to me and opened his hand. Inside was a thick piece of lead, the size of a roll of quarters. "Fishing weight from one of Andy's excursions," he said.

I nodded, impressed but focused on the moving gondola. "Coming up fast." We were still out of range of the gunfire, but Mitch needed to make his move before that changed.

Pressing against the side glass, I honed in on Dad's speeding cable car in the distance. I froze as I stared at it, and made the mistake of looking down. The distance was deadly. I pulled back, second-guessing our plan.

"Listen, Mitch," I said, shooting out the glass sunroof of the cable car and stepping out of the way of the falling shards. "I can't let you do it. I'm making the jump."

As I prepared to grab the edges of the open sunroof, Mitch gripped my arm. "Wait! No way."

"If you don't make it—"

He shook his head violently. "The gap between these cars is at least fifteen feet."

"And?" I asked.

"You won't make it. The long jump record at county this year was only twenty-two feet and that's with a running start. The winner of the standing broad jump was only nine feet."

"Your point. Make it fast."

"My point is," he said, "you'll never clear the distance. Not even close."

"But *you* will?"

"I don't know. But I'm the one who set both those county records."

I held his gaze, desperate but afraid. "It should be me taking this risk, not you."

"No time to argue." Mitch leapt up, grabbed the edges of the sunroof, and pulled himself onto the top of the cable car.

As he looked back down, I handed the gun up to him. "If you don't make this, I'll never forgive myself."

"I'd better make it then," he said with a forced smile.

He tucked the gun into his waistband, and I watched his feet disappear as he crawled carefully to the end of the roof.

From inside the cable car, I could hear the thumping of Mitch getting to his feet and imagined him riding the roof like a surfboard, the wind nearly sucking him off the side.

The crack of distant bullets intensified and another loud bump made me jump.

"I'm okay," he yelled from above.

"Be careful!" I shouted, hoisting myself up just enough to see through the sunroof, unable to listen blindly to him staggering above me.

Mitch bent his knees to keep a low center of gravity. I prayed he was still out of range of the guns, though I knew he wasn't.

My heart flipped in wild patterns at the zip and ping of shots fired, but the fact that he was thousands of feet in the air was a more immediate concern. He moved back to the far edge, trying to give himself as much of a running start as possible. My stomach whirled. I imagined his body plummeting, crashing onto the rocky cliffside on the way down, landing at the bottom. Dead. His skull crushed, his limbs turned at grotesque angles on the ground. I forced myself to stop. Dad's car was less than a hundred feet away.

"You can do this," I whispered to myself as the cable car zoomed toward us, getting closer, Closer, CLOSER.

I lowered down and braced for it, waiting to see Mitch

flying across the gap through the glass windows. My heart beat furiously. I pressed my clasped my hands to my chin and squeezed them so tightly all blood receded from my knuckles. *Please make it.*

Right as the car was about to pass, I heard his running feet hit the roof, each thunk a slowed moment in time. He flew forward, the ground below deliriously distant, and my breath caught.

Make it. Please. Make it.

I pressed my palms to the glass as he stretched the last few feet, but it wasn't enough.

"No!" I cried out as he landed half on, half off the roof of Dad's car. His legs dangled against the glass window and he slapped desperately at the metal.

"Mitch!" I screamed, pounding on the wall of the cable car as he started to slide down. Just as he was about to fall, he found the metal lip of the roof and clamped onto it. A wave of adrenaline and fear screamed through my body.

All I could do was watch. He strained and twisted back, grabbed the roof with two hands and finally secured himself. I bit hard into my cheek as he froze for a moment, pressed against the side of the car.

Finally, he released his right hand, grabbed his gun, then jammed it to the side glass and fired. The window shattered and he fell with the shards inside. I closed my eyes, letting a layer of tension melt from my shoulders for the briefest moment, and rested my head against the cold metal frame of the gondola.

I wanted to keep watching, to make sure they got out as planned, but I didn't have time. As I opened the emergency door of the cable car, the wind blew my hair back and burned my eyes. I dragged Castillo's unconscious body to the edge, hooked another zip-line cable under his shoulders and secured him to my chute harness.

With my foot on the edge of the open door, I had one last thought: would our combined weight be too much for this one-man chute? In training I'd learned what would happen if the chute didn't function properly. The human body dropping thirty-five thousand feet generally took three minutes to hit the ground. Low pressure and lack of oxygen caused the person to lose consciousness. That was, until the last fifty seconds or so, where they'd be jarred back awake in time to see the ground screaming toward them at one hundred and twenty miles per hour.

But then another thought quickly superseded that one...it didn't matter.

I lifted Castillo nearly to his feet, leaned out of the car with him and fell forward. Wind instantly tore at our clothes as we tumbled through the air. I'd done this before, but the terrifying rush never got easier. My heart raced and I panicked, unable to compensate for Castillo's extra weight. As we free-fell toward the ground, Castillo's eyes shot open. The sheer terror in his scream was almost comical. He locked his legs around my waist like a clinging child.

"Calm down!" I shouted over the wind, but his frantic

clawing and climbing was spinning us out of control.

After a few seconds, I managed to twist my arm around his neck, locking him in a sleeper hold until his body went limp. Just in time, I pulled my chute cord and it opened with a loud *thwump.* The recoil was extreme. I cried out, almost losing my grip on Castillo before I scissored my legs tighter and secured him once more. The chute straps strained at the arrest of my descent, sending lancing pain up my spine, but the black rectangular fabric billowed above, slowing us into a glide. Finally, I manipulated one of the handles and got my fall under control.

Below me lay a myriad of river outlets. Off to the left, I spotted my destination: Andy and our boat. I angled the chute and targeted the landing spot.

Hooking my free arm around Castillo to keep him from slipping, I looked up to see Dad and Mitch free-falling too. I reflexively held my breath until both threw their chutes and *thwump, thwump.* They opened.

I blew out a breath. *Almost there.*

It was only then that I remembered Nefasto. I used my free hand to snatch my binoculars and found the base port. It looked like someone had poked an anthill with a stick. The men ran around crazed, and in the center, Nefasto screamed at them and pointed.

Five men stepped to the ledge and aimed at Dad and Mitch. Distant gunfire spiked the air, like bundles of firecrackers. This far out, the shooters were extremely inaccurate. They missed Dad completely, but a couple got lucky and struck Mitch's chute.

I clenched my jaw, waiting for the next wave of bullets, but Nefasto ordered his men to move. They hopped into a line of black SUVs. I exhaled at the momentary relief, then caught sight of Mitch. His chute was shredded. Puddles of open sky formed in the fabric and he began to accelerate.

His chute, which had taken hard shots, began to collapse and flutter. He pulled on the links and risers of the chute trying to stabilize it, but it was no use. Every foot he dropped, the chute got worse. Pieces of fabric flapped in the wind.

Helpless, all I could do was watch. As Mitch dropped faster, the chute disintegrated and sent him into a total free fall. He dropped like a stone and struck the water. Hard.

Seconds later, I dropped on the riverbank with Castillo. I motioned to Andy to get Mitch, but Dad had already jettisoned his chute. He swam toward the circled wake where Mitch landed, and got there just as Mitch surfaced, his face curled in a rictus of pain.

"Is he okay?" I yelled, my voice high-pitched with worry.

As Dad helped Mitch to shore, they headed toward me, and Andy ran up to help.

"Broke his collar bone," Dad answered as he pressed on Mitch's shoulder, around his neck.

Mitch slapped Dad's hand away crying out in agony.

"We need to go." I frantically waved Andy over to help haul Castillo, and we all climbed into the boat.

Andy fired up the engine and Dad palmed his shoulder. "What are you doing here?"

He shrugged. "I had to make sure you came through on the deal you promised."

As an entourage of black Escalades pulled along the nearest road, I caught Andy's eye. "Get us out of here."

CHAPTER TWENTY-FIVE

WITH EVERYONE SECURE, ANDY jammed the throttle down and floored the boat away. It launched forward, nose in the air, until he leveled it out and sped down the large river inlet, heading directly for the ocean.

Mitch tossed the handgun I gave him onto the floor of the boat. "It's empty."

"That's all we have?" Dad asked, grabbing the gun.

I walked to the secret loading compartment of the boat and popped it open to reveal stacks of TAR-21 assault rifles, then opened another compartment full of M33 spherical fragmentation grenades.

Dad's swollen eyebrows lifted slightly. "You guys have been busy."

I shrugged and noticed Castillo shift. He lay bound on the floor of the boat, and though his eyes remained closed, I was sure he was conscious.

"So what's the plan with him?" Dad asked, nodding to his target.

Before I could respond, Andy shouted. "We have trouble!"

Two go-fast boats full of armed men slid in behind us and opened fire. Bullets dimpled the water. I grabbed an assault rifle and tossed one to Dad, who immediately unloaded back. I paused for a moment, taking in the surreal image of the two of us gunning down a common enemy. Things could still go wrong, and having him here shouldn't have made me feel more comfortable, but it did.

Shoulder to shoulder, we fired. Our return hail of bullets disabled one of the boats, which turned off in a cloud of black smoke. Behind us, Mitch came up with a fist full of grenades. He winced from the pain in his collarbone, and handed them to me. I yanked the pins and lobbed them at the pursuing craft.

The river exploded around the trailing boat, sending water into the air, but the third one connected. It disintegrated the bow of the craft, catapulted the men into the air and sprayed them around the river like marionettes with their strings cut. As Andy took a hard left down a small inlet, the large brush grass blurred past, and I saw no sign of any more boats.

"Clear," Andy shouted back as he slowed the engine.

Dad was almost in a trance, staring at Mitch, then me. Shock still registered on his face. He shook his head. "Seeing you two here...I'm just having a hard time wrapping my head around it."

"*You're* having a hard time?" Mitch said sardonically. "Last time I saw you, you were building slides for washing machines."

The boat sped up. "Spoke too soon!" Andy shouted again.

Three more go-fast pursuers zipped out from side inlets, two hundred yards behind. They formed an arrow pattern and made up ground quickly.

Dad unloaded a stream of bullets, then barked at Andy. "We need to go faster."

Andy held his arms out. "The boat is full throttle."

I looked around, my mind racing, something didn't make sense. "These boats are nearly identical," I said. "In fact, if anything, this boat should be a little faster. It's the weight, we're too heavy! Get rid of everything."

I yanked weapons out of the compartments and began tossing them overboard. Dad helped, and together we dumped crates and crates of weapons into the water.

Other than a few automatic rifles, we dumped everything we could find. But it was too late, three chasing boats arrived within range. The men inside opened fire, and Andy took evasive action, desperately dodging the shots.

"Wait," I yelled. "I have an idea." I charged toward Castillo, who was still feigning sleep, and yanked at his shirt. As expected, his eyes snapped open.

I held Castillo out in front of me, and the gunfire ceased.

The boats, however, did not.

Andy took a left, then a quick right, but still couldn't escape. "It's no good. They're still faster. Hang on."

I shoved Castillo in a corner just before Andy jerked the boat into a hard right. We zoomed down a side inlet and headed away from the ocean.

"You're going the wrong way," I shouted over the engine.

"I have lived here all my life, I know these inlets. You trust me, right?"

"Yes, but—" I stopped. "Yes. I trust you."

Andy steered the boat down another path with dangerously shallow water. As he maneuvered in and out, slaloming along the hidden pools, one of the three trailing boats miscalculated and ran aground. The drivers of the other two boats were more skilled and matched Andy turn for turn.

Dad and I fired our semiautomatics, but the boats behind zigzagged so quickly we couldn't connect.

Mitch stepped up between us. "Don't shoot at the boats. Use your fire to force them where you want them to go."

I looked at Dad and got an approving nod. As the boats behind zigged and zagged, we shot giant streams of automatic weapon fire toward the zig. The drivers of both boats instinctively zagged, which was exactly what we wanted them to do. It sent the two boats directly into shallow water. The lead boat ran aground and stopped so suddenly that the other couldn't avoid it. The two vessels smashed into each other and the hulls exploded in a staggering eruption of wood, steel and fiberglass.

Dad looked back at Mitch. "Good thinking, Son."

But the fleeting moment of victory came crashing to an end as four more boats pulled in behind us.

Andy pounded the wheel. "Where do they keep coming from?"

As he zipped back into the main inlet, the ocean became visible ahead.

"The ocean!" I screamed. "We're almost there."

A smile ran across my face, then just as quickly, it evaporated. A hundred yards, dead ahead, completely cutting off our exit to open water was Nefasto. He was in a speed boat, flanked by two large military cruisers on either side. Every boat was full of weapon-wielding gunmen. Together they formed a giant, deadly blockade.

"No..." I said softly, almost to myself.

With the four boats behind and the blockade in front, we were trapped. There were no more inlets to turn down. Andy seemed to have no more tricks up his sleeve. Our escape was thwarted. It was over.

"We were so close," I said, dropping my weapon.

I turned to Mitch, but realized he was distracted. He stood in a complete daze. Shock, I thought. But he stared at something intently. I followed his gaze, and saw one last secret compartment I'd missed. Mitch reached over and popped it open. There, nestled deep inside, were Castillo's custom hand-held missile launchers.

Andy slowed the boat and yelled back. "What do I do?"

Even in the middle of all the chaos, Mitch was transfixed. I pulled out the missile for him and handed it to Dad, but he shook his head.

"This is a new model. I haven't seen these." He looked up at me. "There's no way to know what the blast radius is."

"He'll know," Andy said, pointing at Castillo.

A devilish grin pulled at Castillo's cheeks. He sat hunched in the corner, a madman holding the code to an armed bomb. "Why would I tell you? I'm already dead."

I raised my gun, days of rage boiling over into this moment, but Dad held up a hand, stopping me. "You kill him, we all die."

I let out a heavy breath and turned back. "Didn't the CIA get data from the embassy blast?"

"That's what I'm saying," Dad said, holding up the missile. "That was an older model. An early prototype. This one is completely different. If I fire this one, the blast could take us all out."

"I've seen it," Mitch said. "I've seen this one fired."

Dad's brow drew into a deep wrinkle. "What? Where?"

"Doesn't matter, Tara and I both saw it used in person. I saw the blast radius for myself. I can do the calculations."

"But..."

Mitch motioned out toward the blockade. "I could

guesstimate."

My eyes went wide. "Guesstimate?"

Mitch spun, as if measuring how far away the blockade was. "An educated guess, then. I think it will work. Fire it."

"Mitch..."

He turned to Dad. "People live and die. But as long as they do both things with purpose, there's never much to regret."

Dad's bruised and swollen lips turned up slightly. "That's my line."

"It will work, I know it."

"Least if we go out..." I said, motioning toward Castillo. "...we go out together and the world's a safer place, right?"

Dad shouldered the weapon and looked back at us. "I love you kids."

"Love you," I uttered in that frozen moment before he turned and pulled the trigger. Then, just like that, the missile launched. It cleared the space to the blockade in less than a second and hit Nefasto's boat dead center.

Instantly, the air itself seemed to blur and warp. The missile didn't explode, but rather imploded with such force that it yanked all five boats in the blockade together and vaporized them in a tsunami of swirling debris and shrapnel. I barely had time to take my eyes away from the scene before realizing the outer range of the rebounding blast had indeed reached us. The implosion gripped our boat like a giant hand and yanked it toward the epicenter.

"Hold on," I screamed.

Everyone flattened against the wooden floor of the craft as we were drawn toward the blast. I braced for the crash, expecting the boat to flip and slip into pieces. But just as we were about to get sucked into the fission typhoon, the mini storm lost strength. We flew forward into the dying epicenter, which had weakened dramatically, but were still sling-shotted out the other side. As we exited, the vortex whipped us up and launched our boat another twenty feet in the air. We rocketed through the space for what seemed like eternity before landing hard and skipping like a giant stone across the water. The craft nearly flipped several times, before it slowly, finally, righted itself. Then coasted out to sea.

I pulled myself up and stared back at the wreckage, completely stunned. The tornado of flotsam and jetsam slowed to a stop, the last remains littering the surface of the sloshing waves. A blue-black mushroom cloud of vapor rose into the air like a giant smoke ring before it separated and evaporated.

The drivers of the four boats behind us didn't move. For a brief moment, I thought they might actually continue the hunt. But Dad had managed to keep hold of the missile launcher. He held it up toward them, and they immediately turned around, gunning their boats back the way they came. As they disappeared around the bend, all four of us turned to each other and laughed. The kind of hysterical laughter that tends to come after being nearly vaporized.

Mitch reached out, extended a congratulatory hand. I pushed it aside and wrapped him in a hug.

"Easy," he called out in pain.

I jumped back, wincing as he held his collarbone. "Sorry."

He laughed, and our eyes connected in a moment of pure relief.

"So now what?" Andy asked as he coasted out to sea.

I strode up behind him, but instead of answering his question, I kissed him. Long and hard.

As I pulled back, I caught a glimpse of Dad's confused face. He held up his hand. "I don't wanna know."

I smiled and handed him the cell phone I'd been using. Dad dialed without question. "Sat 14, Agent A, Tango, Zero. Requesting package pick-up."

THE SUN BEAT down from above. Its beams danced on the rolling water, glittering like a trail of stardust. In the back of the boat, Castillo sat sulking. With the Keys visible in the distance, I finally allowed myself to believe we'd made it. I smiled at Dad as we spotted five U.S. Coast Guard RB-M boats in the distance. The big metal crafts headed toward us in a perfect V formation.

"Take her down," Dad said, stepping up next to Andy.

He slowed the boat, eventually coming to a full stop.

The lead Coast Guard vessel slid toward us, and the other four boats flanked each side.

As Mitch tossed a Coast Guardsman a docking rope and knotted the boats together, a large-bellied man with nicely-combed bright red hair stepped on board. He had to be important. He looked too out of place in his gray tweed overcoat.

"Agent Doaks," Dad greeted him.

The agent reached out and they shook hands.

"Harry," Doaks nodded, "little early for a boat ride, don't you think?"

Dad attempted to smile past the bruises on his face. "Never too early."

"Nice to see you're enjoying retirement since leaving the agency." Agent Doaks turned to Castillo and let out a fake gasp. "Oh my gosh, that looks just like Javier Castillo. Do you know the C.I.A.'s been looking all over for this guy?"

Dad's eyebrows rose, as he feigned surprise. "You don't say."

"We've been trying to get him here to America, but Cuba wouldn't cooperate. I'm shocked he would venture into American territory like this. He's wanted here for a litany of offenses. Where'd you find him?"

"He was floating in the middle of the ocean on a raft made out of palm fronds. We probably saved his life, the poor bastard."

Castillo leaned forward and screamed. "That's a lie!

They kidnapped me. I want to be returned to Cuba immediately and demand that they are sent back as well for prosecution."

"I don't know, Mr. Castillo," Agent Doaks said, giving Dad a wink. "Extradition's a tricky thing."

With this, Agent Doaks grabbed Castillo and shoved him toward the waiting hands of several Coast Guardsmen. He stepped back onto the Coast Guard boat, and turned to Dad. "You wanna lift?"

"Nah," Dad waved him off. "We'll take her in ourselves. Logging a little family time."

Agent Doaks nodded, rocking back on his heels in a hunkered, thinking posture. "All right. Just leave the boat someplace we can find it."

At the agent's command, Mitch untied the ropes and all the Coast Guard crafts took off at once. As they slowly disappeared into the distance, the red-hot sun passed behind a thick wall of clouds, burning into it like the end of a lit cigarette.

EPILOGUE

I PEEKED THROUGH THE blinds of our kitchen window. Mitch was practicing shooting hoops one-handed in the driveway. His collarbone had mostly healed, but his right arm was still locked in a sling. Even using one hand, the ball swished through the net, hit the garage door and bounced back to him.

After weeks of being home, it still seemed bizarre to be surrounded by such normalcy. But it also felt good. I popped through the front door and walked out of the house holding two large glasses with green goop in them. I handed one to Mitch, and he dropped the ball to take it.

"Thanks," he said.

"This stuff's actually not horrible. You sure it's good for me?" I asked, taking a sip.

"It'll put hair on your chest."

"Great. Just what every girl wants."

Mitch guzzled nearly half the glass, then ran his free forearm across his lips. "How's your boyfriend doing in there?"

"Boyfriend..." I repeated the word with a nod. "Still getting used to that."

Mitch smiled. "Is he whipping us up some dinner?"

"Totally. I never pegged him as a chef, but that guy was born for it. You should see him in there. Pots boiling, pans smoking, meat and vegetables flying around. It's like a freakin' circus."

"Any news from up top?" he asked. "Dad come through with his papers?"

"Yup. Andy just signed them. He is officially allowed to be here."

Just then a car roared down the road and pulled into the driveway across the street. The BMW convertible lurched to a stop. Nora sat in the passenger seat, and Jake hung his muscular arm out the window, bobbing his head to a reverberating techno beat.

"Speaking of boyfriends," Mitch said.

"Ahh," I watched Jake as he pumped his fist to the music. "I really hate him. You're so much better for her."

"Somehow I don't think she's aware of that."

"Maybe you should *tell* her," I said, patting him on the back. "Dinner in ten."

As I slipped back into the house, I couldn't help but keep the door open just a hair. I watched through the crack to see if he'd take my advice. Mitch looked back across the street. The BMW was already backing out into the road.

Jake glared at him. "The hell you starin' at, pissant?"

Mitch didn't budge. Instead, he offered a big smile. "Just admiring your puka shell necklace, Bro." Mitch gave him a hard wink. "Sweet."

Jake scowled, held up his middle finger and floored the car away.

I was about to close the door, but Mitch noticed Nora fumbling with her keys. He set down his glass and walked slowly toward her, as if in a trance.

"Nora!" he finally blurted out.

As she turned, Mitch jogged over. I couldn't hear what they were saying, but she squinted at him, and the smile didn't leave her face.

Then, without warning, he leaned in and kissed her. I put a hand over my mouth, probably more surprised than she was, and watched as she actually kissed him back. I smiled to myself as he sealed the deal and turned with a stupid grin on his face.

He sprinted back across the street heading straight for the house. Embarrassed I'd been spying, I closed the door quickly, trying to find something I could pretend to be doing, but he burst into the living room catching me doing nothing. He leaned against the wall and rubbed his face with his working hand.

I gave him a thumbs up, unable to hide my excitement.

"Were you watching the whole time?"

I winced. "I'm sorry. I couldn't look away. I thought

it was gonna be a train wreck, but you totally rocked it."

"Really?"

"That was something out of a movie. Beyond good."

"Thanks." Mitch couldn't shake his stupid smile.

I threw my arm around his shoulder, which made him grimace in pain. He walked with me to the kitchen, where Andy was moving from counter to counter like a whirling dervish. He ran around, stirring some things, chopping others.

"Is there anything we can do to help?" I asked.

Andy ran up and gave me a kiss. "No, no, leave the master to his work. I set the table outside. Tonight, we eat al fresco."

As Andy shooed us away, we headed through the sliding glass doors where Dad waited by an outdoor table. He had a large bottle in his hand, and as we walked out into the yard, he popped the cork.

"Sit down you two," he said. "I got us a little sparkling cider."

Mitch laughed. "Ahh, nice. The hard stuff."

We took a seat at the table and Dad poured us each a glass. Then he raised his for a toast. He took a deep breath, as if in preparation for a big, grand, emotional speech. But instead, said only two words. "To family."

"To family," Mitch and I said back, in unison.

"I love you guys. What you both did for me was, well..." he sighed. "Don't ever, *ever* do that again."

As we all clinked glasses and took a sip, Sasha exited

the house.

"Evening, everyone," she said, uncomfortably brushing a piece of hair back into her tight bun.

My heart stopped. She hadn't been back since we'd returned, and it seemed almost too good to be true that we'd get off scot free for what we did.

Dad turned to me and gave me a look, as if he could read my mind. "Take it easy, Tara. We're on the same team." He walked forward, greeting her with a kiss, and a long hug. "So glad you came."

After their shared moment, she moved toward the table, briefly flashing her white smile. "I guess there's no need to be discreet," she said, tossing a dark brown envelope in front of us.

"What's that?" Mitch asked.

"A job," Dad answered.

Before I could respond, Andy yelled from the kitchen. "Okay, now I could use some help. Uhhh, and rapido, por favor."

Sasha held up her hand. "I've got it. We met on my way in."

She squeezed Dad's shoulders and headed back into the house. Mitch stared at me, then down at the envelope.

"The next extraction target?" I finally asked.

Dad nodded and shrugged. "Gotta keep the lights on."

I couldn't quite tell what he was thinking, but there was definite uncertainty in his eyes.

"Look, I won't lie to you," he filled the silence. "I do get satisfaction out of it. But it's more than that. With all the extradition issues and rogue governments, most of these guys aren't even hiding. These are some of the worst criminals on the planet. Murderers, arms dealers, drug kingpins. All out there, just living it up. Free as birds. Thinking they can't be touched. We can't let those kind of criminals just go free..."

A single word stood out to me as I listened: *We.*

My heart began to pound at the thought of taking on criminals together. Reliving the moment when we turned Castillo over to Doaks made my body buzz with a familiar thrill I'd come to find comfort in. It was possible, "extracting" could be our family business. Maybe all I'd learned didn't have to go to waste. It could be my calling, give my life purpose. I could make a living doing something good.

"Only thing the FBI or the CIA can do is farm it out," Dad continued, though I hadn't been listening. "Throw money at the situation. Pay extractors like me," he said and winked. "Someone's gotta do it."

"Wait," I said. "How much?"

Dad looked up. "How much what?"

"Money, for each extraction. What numbers we talkin' here?"

He laughed. "Depends how bad the bad guy is. Low six figures. Sometimes more."

I raised my eyebrows at Mitch and followed his gaze to the brown envelope. Suddenly, we were both lunging for it.

"Hey," Dad said. "Be careful with that."

I ripped the envelope out of Mitch's hands. "Age before beauty."

He rolled his eyes, then watched as I popped it open, emptied the contents and pulled out surveillance photos of the next target. I stopped breathing when I saw the face and fell back into my chair like I'd just been shot.

"What?" Dad asked.

"The target...for the next extraction job..."

"What?" Mitch insisted. "Spit it out."

I spun the photo around so they could both see it. "It's Mom."

ABOUT THE AUTHORS

JOE GAZZAM was born in Baltimore, MD, grew up in Fort Lauderdale, FL and graduated from the University of Florida. He's been a working screenwriter for the last fifteen years, living in Southern California with his wife and young son. And while he loves writing for film and television, books have always been his true passion.

WWW.JOEGAZZAM.COM

JESSICA THERRIEN spent most of her life in the small town of Chilcoot, CA, high up in the Sierra Nevada Mountains. In this town of nearly 100 residents, with no street lights or grocery stores, there was little to do but find ways to be creative. She is the author of the #1 best-selling YA series, *Children of the Gods*, which has been translated and sold around the world. Jessica currently lives in Southern California with her husband and their three children.

JOIN *the* INSIDER'S CLUB for
exclusive sneak peeks, cover reveals, new release
announcements & FREEBIES!

WWW.JESSICATHERRIENBOOKS.COM

ALSO BY JOE GAZZAM

Jason Holden has been on thin ice since his mother died. Capping off a burglary and bar fight with a brutal car wreck, the seventeen-year-old finds himself firmly on the wrong side of the law.

His behavior isn't winning him any points with his father, who happens to be the state governor. So when Governor Holden learns of a program for troubled youth, he jumps at the chance to deal with Jason's outbursts while cementing his position for being tough on crime.

The program is a radical exercise designed to frighten teens from a life of crime. It's called "Scared Straight," and takes them into the heart of Blackenbush Maximum Security Penitentiary.

Jason, along with a group of hardened juvenile delinquents, quickly comes face to face with some of the most extreme convicts the state has ever seen. But what's designed as an exercise becomes all too real as a prisoner take-over comes to fruition. Before long the entire penitentiary is under siege, surrounded by feds and overrun with violent lifers loose from their cells.

Jason, trapped in the middle of the chaos, will have to trust in the most unlikely person— Karl Rix, a convict with his own body count. Between them, they just might find a way to save their skin and even a bit of redemption. But at what cost?

ALSO BY JESSICA THERRIEN

The Children of the Gods Series

The Descendants have waited long enough for freedom...

Elyse knows what it means to keep a secret. She's been keeping secrets her whole life. Two, actually. First, that she ages five times slower than average people, so that while she looks eighteen years old, she's closer to eighty. Second, that her blood has a mysterious power to heal. For Elyse, these things don't make her special. They make life dangerous. After the death of her parents, she's been careful to keep her secret as closely guarded as possible. Now, only one other person in the world knows about her age and ability. Or so she thinks. Elyse is not the only one keeping secrets. There are others like her all over the world, descendants of the very people the Greeks considered gods. She is one of them, and they have been waiting for her for a long time. Some are waiting for her to put an end to centuries of traditions that have oppressed their people under the guise of safeguarding them. Others are determined to keep her from doing just that. But for Elyse, the game is just beginning—and she's not entirely willing to play by their rules.

"A riveting page-turner. Jessica Therrien broke my heart into a million pieces—and then put it back together again. This book will haunt and uplift readers long after they turn the last page."

—*KAT ROSS, best-selling author of The Midnight Sea*

CARRY ME HOME is a work of fiction inspired by the true story of a teenage girl's involvement in several Mexican gangs in San Jose and Los Angeles. The members of her crew call her, Guera, Spanish for "white girl" and it doesn't take long for her to get lost in their world of guns and drugs.

* * *

Lucy and Ruth are country girls from a broken home. When they move to the city with their mother, leaving behind their family ranch and dead-beat father, Lucy unravels.

They run to their grandparents' place, a trailer park mobile home in the barrio of San Jose. Lucy's barrio friends have changed since her last visit. They've joined a gang called VC. They teach her to fight, to shank, to beat a person unconscious and play with guns. When things get too heavy, and lives are at stake, the three girls head for LA, seeking a better life.

But trouble always follows Lucy. She befriends the wrong people, members of another gang, and every bad choice she makes drags the family into her dangerous world.

Told from three points of view, the story follows Lucy down the rabbit hole, along with her mother and sister as they sacrifice dreams and happiness, friendships and futures. Love is waiting for all of them in LA, but pursuing a life without Lucy could mean losing her forever.

ACKNOWLEDGMENTS

A big thank you to Laurie and Rex Gazzam, Joe's wife and son, as well as Brian, Matthew, J.J., and Annabelle Therrien, Jessica's husband and children. We are both very thankful to have families who encourage and support our writing.

Many thanks to literary agents, Beth Miller and Suzie Townsend, for the kind words and brilliant advice.

And thank you READERS of our books! We're so grateful for you.

From Jessica:

A huge thanks to my writing partner, business partner, and best friend, Holly Kammier, for EVERYTHING. What would I ever do without you? To Lacey Impellizeri for your tiny bursts of marketing wisdom and continuous support. To Kat Ross for reading and editing early drafts and providing amazing feedback. To my mom, Janet, for always reading and loving everything I write. And to my in-laws, Ron and Mary Jane, for being my constant sounding board.

www.ingramcontent.com/pod-product-compliance
Lightning Source LLC
Chambersburg PA
CBHW030527310726
48979CB00010B/1831/J

9781947392755